Dad Plopped a Plate of Pale White Lumps of Different Sizes in Front of Me.

The harder I stared, the more they seemed to stare back at me.

I pushed a couple of the lumps around with my fork. "Dad, how come they look so funny? They look like eyeballs."

"Don't be silly. They may look funny, but they're good for you. They're scrambled eggs made with just the whites—no yolks. No yolks—no cholesterol. And cooked lightly in a no-stick pan with no fat. Healthy eggs, I call them. My own invention. Eat up, Murphy."

I looked around for help, but there was none. He stood over me while I mashed one of the lumps with my fork. The white squished up through the prongs. I closed my eyes, stabbed a lump, and put it into my mouth. I swallowed quickly without chewing.

Dad hung over me until I had finished half the plate. "Not bad, huh, Murphy?"

I just nodded.

It was pretty depressing to realize I couldn't even count on breakfast to be normal anymore.

Eyeballs
for
Breakfast

M. M. RAGZ

A MINSTREL® BOOK

PUBLISHED BY POCKET BOOKS

New York   London   Toronto   Sydney   Tokyo   Singapore

A MINSTREL PAPERBACK *ORIGINAL*

A Minstrel Book published by
POCKET BOOKS, a division of Simon & Schuster Inc.
1230 Avenue of the Americas, New York, NY 10020

ISBN: 0-671-73339-7

First Minstrel Books printing August 1990

10 9 8 7 6 5 4 3 2

A MINSTREL BOOK and colophon are registered trademarks of Simon & Schuster Inc.

Printed in the U.S.A.

With Love to
Phil
and my sons Michael, Kenny and P.T.
for so many reasons

Eyeballs
for
Breakfast

CHAPTER ONE

Peter Patterson, my best friend, was about to get himself into big trouble. Our class was right in the middle of a current events activity period, working in small groups writing news stories and pasting down pictures to go with them. I was working with Peter and a couple of other guys. In the group right in front of us was a new girl in our class who considered herself Ms. Marvelous—Ashley Douglas. Peter was reaching out to yank on Ashley's long braid, and I had to work fast. I grabbed his wrist.

"Don't do it, Peter," I whispered. "It's not worth it."

"Let go, Murphy," he whispered back as I fought to keep his hand inches away from the dark, thick rope of hair that hung almost to Ashley's waist. "I'm not doing anything."

"Yeah, sure, Peter. You're just getting yourself into big trouble, that's all. You can thank me later."

"Since when are *you* such a goody-goody?" he asked.

"Since now. It's still only September, you know. You want to make a good impression on our new teacher, don't you?"

While we quietly struggled, Mrs. Phister, who was working at her desk, looked up and raised an eyebrow at us. Peter and I smiled at her and he reluctantly lowered his hand. Mrs. Phister went back to work.

"I guess you're right, Murphy. But that Ashley thinks she's such a big deal. She acts like she's real special, and that gives me a pain. I'd just like to see her get it one time—good. Come on, let's get back to work."

But I stood there looking at Ashley. Her back was turned to me, and she was working and talking with a couple of other girls. She never even realized that I had practically saved her life.

Her long braid was fascinating. I was almost hypnotized watching it dance and shine as she talked. I slowly reached forward to touch it. I wanted to know if it would feel as nice as it looked. Suddenly Ashley swung around and glared at me.

"Keep your hands to yourself, Murphy Darinzo," she said loud enough for everyone around to hear. "I don't want you wiping your grimy hands on my clean hair." She flipped her head around, practically swatting me in the face with the braid. The other girls laughed.

At first I was embarrassed. I felt like an ant someone had squished on the sidewalk and left there for everyone else to stomp on. Then I got mad and wanted revenge.

I looked around. Mrs. Phister was still working at her

desk and everyone else was busy in their groups. A big gallon jug of paste was next to me on an empty desk behind Ashley. I carefully slid the big jar full of gray gunk right behind Ashley and her fancy braid.

With one quick movement I plunged the braid splat into the middle of the sticky gray gop. Suddenly—*smack!* Ashley Douglas spun around and slapped me right in the face—hard—and it hurt. Then, to make matters worse, she started hollering at me—loud.

"Murphy," she shrieked in my face. She got so close I could see myself in her dark blue eyes and smell the peanut butter on her breath. "Look at my hair. How am I ever going to get this paste out of my braid? You're such a . . . a child!" The way she said "child" hurt more than her slap.

By now, everyone else in class had circled around us and I felt trapped. Ashley's long dark braid was dripping with gooey gray paste, and kids were pointing and laughing and asking what had happened. I think they were waiting for Ashley to haul off and smack me again. In fact, that's exactly what I was waiting for, too.

I closed my eyes. When I opened them, I was looking at Mrs. Phister, who had placed herself between me and Ashley.

"Murphy Darinzo! Are you responsible for this mess?" Mrs. Phister was pointing at Ashley's dripping braid.

"Not entirely. I can explain. Really . . . I . . ."

"Murphy, just answer the question. Did you or did you not dunk Ashley's braid in that big jar of paste?"

"I did, but—"

"No *buts*. I am absolutely shocked by your behavior. You, young man, are going to the principal's office. Don't move from that spot until I write you a note to take to Dr. Harder."

She looked around. "The rest of you—back to work. And someone help Ashley clean up that braid."

Ashley stood there glaring at me while Steffie Whiffet, a sad-looking little girl who hardly ever said anything, scurried around getting paper towels and wiping Ashley's braid. Steffie always hung around Ashley and her friends. They talked to her sometimes, but mostly they ignored her.

How had I gotten myself into this mess? Me—Murphy Darinzo—the all-time good student and good kid. With Ashley around it was easy. That girl could get on my nerves faster than nails across a blackboard.

Mrs. Phister came over, handed me the note, and pointed a very long, very polished fingernail toward the door. I wanted to explain, but I knew it was hopeless. For the first time in my entire life, I was in big trouble and being sent to the principal's office for it. And all because of a stupid girl's dumb braid.

CHAPTER TWO

I tried to make it a long walk to the office. I stopped for a drink. I read a bulletin board that had a big green map of China with trade routes marked in red on it. I tried to start a conversation with a custodian who was swishing a dirty mop in a lonesome corner, but he just grunted and kept mopping. I guess he wasn't interested in trade with China.

When I got to the office, I was told to have a seat. "Dr. Harder will be right with you, young man," the secretary said. She looked at me curiously. Mrs. Phister must have called them on the PA as soon as I walked out of the door, so Dr. Harder, as well as the whole office staff, must have known what a troublemaker I had become.

I tried not to worry and fidget while I was waiting. I was in enough trouble. I fished into my pants pocket and pulled out two big pieces of bubble gum. I carefully unwrapped them, stuck the wrappers back in my pocket, and, pretending I was yawning, sneaked the gum into my mouth.

Chewing gum wasn't allowed in school. But once in a while when I was bored or restless, I needed a piece of gum to calm my nerves. Bubble gum made me even calmer, so I always kept a big supply on hand.

I had chewed most of the gritty sugar out of the gum when the secretary said shrilly, "Young man, Dr. Harder wants you in her office—*now!*"

I hustled into Dr. Harder's office, remembering at the last minute to take the big wad of gum out of my mouth. I didn't know what to do with it, so I shoved it into my pocket. It kept sticking to my fingers and coming back out, so I rubbed it in deep. I'd figure out how to explain the mess to Mom later. I'd rather face Mom with a messy pocket than Dr. Harder with a whole mouthful of gum.

Dr. Harder was a dignified, quiet lady who always lectured us on "proper behavior and manners for the boys and girls of Westford Elementary."

She studied me and the note I gave her for a long time while I stood in front of her desk breaking out in what my mom calls a "panic attack"—every part of me, right down to my toes, was breaking into a sweat.

"Murphy," she said finally, putting her elbows on her desk and pressing her palms together like she was praying. I knew she wanted to make a stern impression on me— and she was succeeding.

"Murphy. I have little to say to you. I am disappointed in your behavior. I know it will never happen again. I will not call your parents—this time. And since it will *never* happen again, I will *never* have to call them. Is that clear?"

Clear as fresh rainwater. She was letting me off the hook. I started to breathe more and sweat less. Since my voice didn't seem to be working, I nodded—a lot. And fast.

Halfway through my head-bobbing act she raised one index finger and pointed at me. "You are a member of this school's gifted program. You are one of the brightest students in your class. Therefore, you are expected to act as maturely as you are expected to think. What you did in class today is unbecoming of any student in Westford Elementary School. I am ashamed of you."

She took a deep breath, shook her head slowly, and continued. "You, of all people, should know better. Both your parents are teachers at Westford High School. They have brought you up to respect education. It is only for their sake that I will not call—this time."

She paused—for emphasis, I'm sure. I don't think she really expected me to answer. For sure I wasn't going to try. Besides, when an adult takes a break in a lecture—parents or teachers—all you have to do is wait about five seconds and they'll start to talk again anyway. My older brother Tony taught me that little trick and it has saved me a lot of wasted words and gotten me out of some tough situations.

Sure enough, a few seconds later she said, "And especially since Ashley Douglas is new to this school, and also in the gifted group with you. I expect you to act accordingly."

I knew it was time to leave because all of a sudden

she started to get busy with a bunch of papers. She looked up once as if she were wondering why I was still sitting there, so I said "thank you," about ten times and backed out of her office.

The last bell signaling the end of the day rang as I walked out of the office. Kids were streaming down the hall in a big swarm, anxious to get out into the fresh air. I didn't want to bump into Ashley, so I ducked into the boys' room to hide until I was sure no one would be left in my classroom. Then I could go back and get my books.

I passed the time practicing faces in one of the mirrors. I lowered my eyebrows and tightened my lips for my "tough" look. Then I sucked in my cheeks and rolled my eyes up for my "who are you kidding" look. The last was my "cool" look—just me looking at me. I whipped my comb out of my pocket and wet it because my shaggy blond hair usually made me look like a sheepdog. I slicked it back, but I knew it'd be in my face again as soon as it dried.

When I was sure the coast was clear, I walked back to my room to get my book bag and homework. The classroom was empty, except for Peter, who was leaning up against the wall munching on an apple. We always walked home together, but I didn't think he'd wait.

"Hey, Murph," he said when he saw me. "What happened? I thought you were into making good impressions. Too bad you got caught."

And I thought no one had been watching. "Why didn't you stop me? I stopped you, remember?"

8

He laughed. "And spoil all my fun? You sure got Ashley good. But then, Ashley got you pretty good, too. Does your face still sting?"

I wasn't in the mood for talking about it. I stuffed my books into my book bag and grabbed my lunch bag out of my desk. I always saved a snack to eat on the way home.

The bag was empty.

I looked up at Peter, who was enjoying his apple. "That's my apple, Peter. You stole my apple."

He munched for a while and tossed the core into the basket. "Yeah, Murphy. I know. But I wasn't sure you'd be coming back and I didn't want your apple to stink up your desk overnight. So I ate it. You can thank me later."

I considered punching him out and then thanking him, but Peter is as big as me. Besides, I didn't have the energy.

"Thanks a whole big bunch, Peter. You are a true friend." I tried to sound sarcastic.

"Hey! I'm the guy who waited for you, Murphy. That's more than I can say for anyone else. They all figured you'd be banished to Russia for what you did."

He was right. As we walked home together Peter made me sound like a hero. "I told you what I think of Ashley. She thinks she's so special. I was hoping you'd get away with it."

"Yeah," I agreed. But I wasn't feeling too terrific. Ashley would probably never talk to me again. Not that I cared, but I didn't want anyone to think I was a jerk—not even Ashley.

When we got to Peter's house, he said, "Want to come in for a snack? I do owe you one."

I was all set to accept until he said, "Wonder what your dad and mom are going to do to you when they find out. They always do, you know."

Suddenly I wasn't hungry anymore. If Peter was right and they did find out, I'd be in for it. Mom, the English teacher, would hand me a notebook and make me write why I did it and how I felt about it. Dad was completely different. He's a physical education teacher and a coach, so he handles problems more physically. He'd just start hollering and give me a couple of hundred push-ups or sit-ups to do to work off all my extra energy. That's his idea of how to keep kids out of trouble.

This day was definitely not going down on my list of "Best Days of my Life."

CHAPTER THREE

The next morning I had a real problem getting my eyes to open—they must have been glued together. Or maybe I just didn't want to face Ashley and Mrs. Phister.

Mom was standing at the foot of my bed, jiggling my feet. "Murphy—aren't you up yet? Come on, Murphy. It's not like you to have trouble getting up."

That was true. I was usually up before everyone else. But I had spent a night full of dreams fighting with Ashley, running from Mrs. Phister and Dr. Harder, and doing push-ups. I was exhausted.

"Mom, I don't feel so good. I'd better stay home. It's Friday, and we don't do much on Fridays, anyway." I rolled over and tried to get lost under the covers.

She sat on the edge of the bed, rolled me over, and eyed me suspiciously. "Did something happen at school that I should know about?" I tried not to let her look me in the eye, because I think she could read my mind. I closed my eyes. "Besides," she continued. "This is

11

only the end of September. What do you mean you don't do much on Fridays?"

"I'm telling you, Mom. Mrs. Phister isn't a Friday person. She'll probably show some dumb movie. She does that all the time."

She stood up very tall and very straight. "Okay, Murphy. You stay home."

I could hardly believe my ears. I opened my eyes and gave Mom a big smile.

She wasn't smiling back. "And I'll call Dr. Harder this morning and find out why a teacher doesn't have her class working on Fridays."

I pushed the covers back. "That's okay, Mom. I'm feeling a little better. And I just remembered that Mrs. Phister said something about a math quiz."

Mom didn't say anything. Just bent down and kissed me and left.

As I dressed, I started to look forward to breakfast. That seemed to be the most normal thing in my life right now. Good old cornflakes and milk. Even when life seemed to toss me upside down, I knew I could count on breakfast to make me feel right.

When I got down to the kitchen, Dad was standing at the stove whistling and cooking. Mom was muttering over a stack of school papers that she was busily correcting while she was drinking coffee. My two brothers were eating.

Mom looked up, saw me, and shoved one of the papers she was correcting into my face.

"Murphy. Quick. Look at this sentence. What's the predicate?"

Mom takes her job seriously, and if she is into predicates, the whole family is into predicates.

I mumbled something and sort of pointed to a part of the sentence. She waved the paper in the air and said to Dad, "See? See what I have to put up with? Even Murphy can pick out a simple predicate. So how come my ninth graders can't?"

Dad stopped whistling and tried to look very serious. "Murphy's just exceptionally bright," he said to Mom. "After all, he is your son."

She just nodded and buried her head back into her papers.

I walked over to Dad, figuring I might pick up another compliment, when he pointed his spatula at me and asked, "How do you want your eggs, Murphy? A good breakfast fuels you up for the day. Keeps the old engine running."

I looked over at the table and saw both of my brothers seriously concentrating on their bowls of cereal. They're a lot older than me—Tony's nineteen and Ken's twenty-two. Tony was going to Westford Community College and Ken was out of college working full time. I kept thinking they'd move out, but Dad loved having all his boys at home.

"That's okay, Dad," I said, walking toward my chair between them. "I'll join Tony and Kenny in a dish of cereal."

As I reached between them for the cornflakes, Ken grabbed me by the arm and whispered in my ear, "Listen, Murph. You're going to hurt Dad's feelings. Have some eggs, will you?"

13

"But you guys aren't having eggs."

He squeezed my arm a little harder. "Have eggs, Murphy. We told Dad you'd be happy to have him cook for you." His grip tightened. Tony reached under the table, grabbed my leg, and also started to squeeze.

I figured Dad's eggs would be better than bruised arms and legs. "Okay, Dad. Scrambled eggs for me."

Within minutes, Dad plopped a plate of pale white lumps of different sizes in front of me. I looked closer. I guessed they were eggs, but they were the whitest, gooiest, lumpiest eggs I had ever seen. The harder I stared, the more they seemed to stare back at me.

Dad was standing over me, waiting for me to start shoveling them into my mouth.

I pushed a couple of the lumps around with my fork. "Dad, how come they look so funny? They look like eyeballs."

"Don't be silly. They may look funny, but they're good for you. They're scrambled eggs made with just the whites—no yolks, No yolks—no cholesterol. And cooked lightly in a no-stick pan with no fat. Healthy eggs, I call them. My own invention. Eat up, Murphy."

I looked around for help. Mom was still correcting papers furiously and sipping coffee. Tony and Ken were both staring hard into their cereal bowls and trying not to laugh—but no one, not even those two, ever laughed at Dad.

He stood over me while I mashed one of the lumps with my fork. The white squished up through the prongs. I took a little tiny bite. It didn't really taste disgusting. In fact, it had no taste at all. If I just didn't have to

14

look. I closed my eyes, stabbed around at my plate, speared a lump, and put it in my mouth. I swallowed quickly without chewing.

Dad hung over me until I had finished half the plate. "Not bad, huh, Murphy?" I just nodded.

Mom finally finished her last paper, stacked them into a neat pile, and looked over at me. "Hi, Murphy," she said, smiling. "Glad to see you're feeling better." She looked at the few blobs of egg left on my dish. "What's that mess you're eating?"

"Very healthy eggs, Mom." And I pointed toward Dad, who was cleaning up the stove.

"It's so nice of your father to help out when I have so much schoolwork. Now hurry up and finish. And here's a dollar for hot lunch. I hope you don't mind—it was too late to make sandwiches."

"Thanks, Mom," I said as I gulped down the last of the lumps.

"Murphy, don't eat any junk," my father said. "You don't want to ruin your breakfast."

I could feel my stomach rumble. "Don't worry, Dad. Nothing could do that."

It was pretty depressing to realize I couldn't even count on breakfast to be normal anymore.

CHAPTER FOUR

I practically ran the half mile to Peter's house. Maybe if I was lucky I could get something to eat over there. I could tell that egg whites weren't going to last me until lunch.

Mrs. Patterson answered the door. "Peter's just finishing breakfast, Murphy. You're early this morning."

"Yes, ma'am." I watched hungrily as she picked up a plate with some dried-looking toast and started to walk toward the garbage. "You throwing that toast away?"

She hesitated and held the plate in front of me. "It was a little too dark for Peter."

"I love dark toast," I said, snatching it off the plate. I knew she'd think my family didn't feed me or something, but I was too hungry to worry about it.

I sat down with Peter, crunching on the hard toast, trying to make it last. It was almost burned, but it tasted pretty good after eyeball-white eggs. Peter was working away at pancakes and bacon—with lots of butter and syrup.

16

I tried to make conversation to keep my mind off food. And even though I didn't want to talk about Ashley, I couldn't get her off my mind. "So what do you think, Peter? Think she'll ever think I'm anything but a jerk?"

He was chomping away on his pancakes and bacon. My stomach was grumbling, and I was getting annoyed that he didn't seem too worried about my problems—with Ashley or my stomach.

"How come you're so interested in what a girl thinks?" he asked between bites.

"Who's interested? Not me! Girls are just dumb. They only mess things up and act silly and stupid. I didn't like them before, and I'm not going to start now."

Peter shoved another strip of bacon into his mouth. That left two on his plate. He scratched his head with his fork handle and said, "You know, now that I think about it, I guess you're right."

"You bet I'm right. Girls are a pain."

"No, Murphy. I meant about Ashley. Too bad you blew it. I think she liked you, and she is kind of pretty."

I couldn't believe what I was hearing. "You said she was a pain. Now you call her pretty? Pretty ugly, you mean. You think she's pretty? With that funny long hair and those blue eyes and that little mouth? That's pretty? You need glasses, Peter? Or just your head examined? You think that's pretty? Let me tell you—"

"If you don't care about her, what are you making such a big deal for?"

That made me just shut my mouth and think about changing the subject.

17

Peter burped, rubbed his mouth on his sleeve, and said, "Boy, am I stuffed." I was concentrating on the two pieces of bacon left on his plate. "Murphy, want this bacon? It's a little burnt around the edges."

"I thought you'd never ask. Thanks, Peter. You're a good friend." I scooped up the bacon and stuffed it into my mouth. No sense nibbling on it—I needed a whole mouthful of food.

"Listen, Murphy. If you want to make up with Ashley, why not apologize? Send her a note. Maybe with some flowers or candy. That's what my father does when Mom's mad at him."

"I'm not walking to school with a bunch of flowers, Peter. But candy . . . that's not a bad idea. Got any?"

"Nope. I just give advice. You find your own candy. Come on. Let's go. We're going to be late."

We got to school before the first bell rang. Iggy Sands, his red hair cut like a stiff brush, was in the middle of a bunch of the guys, bragging as usual and showing off. He got in trouble more than anyone else in my class because he was always fooling around and playing jokes on the other kids. Mrs. Phister sometimes had to spend extra time with kids like Iggy, but I don't think he was dumb. He just fooled around so much that he never had time to learn. So he always needed extra help. But we were pretty good friends.

He was shoving a fancy little box into his dirty yellow book bag.

"Hey, Iggy," I said, walking into school with him. "What's in the box?"

He didn't answer right away, as if he was trying to think of a joke or something smart to say. When we got into class, he looked around like he had a big secret and said, "Just some candy, Murphy. Want to see?"

I couldn't believe it. This was going to be my lucky day. He pulled the little box out, opened it quickly, and showed me three pieces of candy wrapped in fancy green-and-pink foil.

"Iggy. Quick. Let me have a piece. Please?"

"Why should I? What's in it for me?"

Good question. I started to dig through my pockets. All I had was some bubble gum, my comb, and my lunch money, and I had to be pretty desperate to give up lunch.

I was pretty desperate. "I'll give you a quarter, Iggy. But I don't have change. I only have my lunch money."

"Then that's what it'll cost you, Murphy. One piece— one dollar. Take it or leave it."

He was about to put the box away when Ashley walked into the room. She looked at me for a long time, then stuck her chin up in the air and turned away.

"Iggy, I'll take it. I probably won't be hungry at lunch anyway." I could feel my stomach rumbling, but I couldn't go through life feeling like a jerk.

"Okay, Murphy. Here it is. You'll never forget this one. The taste is guaranteed."

I didn't bother to ask what he meant. Iggy always talked in riddles anyway.

We still had a few minutes before the class started. I pulled out a piece of paper and worked on a note.

"Dear Ashley. Sorry about the mess. Hope this will

make up for it." I was about to sign "Love, Murphy" but decided against it. I wanted a friend, not a girlfriend. And I certainly didn't want Ashley to get the wrong idea.

I made sure no one was looking and slipped the note with the piece of candy on top of it into her desk.

The day dragged on. I stayed in our classroom during lunch and studied, trying to keep my mind off the hollow hole in my stomach. After lunch I started to worry. Ashley must have found the note and candy, but she seemed to be colder than ever. Maybe she was just playing it cool.

Our last hour of the day was the reading period. Mrs. Phister was giving special attention to a small group of kids, and the rest of the class were quietly doing work sheets. Six of us who were in the gifted group were working on a special lesson together, looking up words in the dictionary. Mrs. Phister had put us into two groups and I had hoped to team up with Ashley, but I ended up with Greg and Michael. Ashley was working with Jennifer and Deanna.

Just before the last bell rang, Deanna came over and slipped a note into my hand. "Ashley said to give this to you," she whispered. "Don't read it till you get home."

I looked over at Ashley, who was looking at me, smiling the biggest, most friendly smile I had ever seen.

Suddenly her note felt like a hot coal in my hand. Maybe she was accepting my apology. Maybe she wanted to be friends. Then I had an awful thought—maybe it was a love note. My hands started to sweat and then I was afraid the sweat would make the ink all blurry and I wouldn't be able to read the note. I shoved it into my pocket where it would be safe until after school.

Everyone was in a hurry to get out of the room as soon as the bell rang. After all, you had to be nuts to hang around on a Friday afternoon.

"Murphy," yelled Peter. "Hurry up. Michael's coming over to my house. We're waiting for you. What's the matter?"

The matter was that I needed some privacy to read Ashley's note.

"Go ahead. I'll catch up with you. Mom wanted me to talk to Mrs. Phister about something." I watched Peter leave.

Mrs. Phister looked up. "Murphy, can I help you with something?"

"No, ma'am. I just thought I'd clean out my desk." I turned my back to her and slid the note out of my pocket. It was damp and crumpled as I opened it up.

"Dearest Murphy," it said in a very curved and flowery script. It was so fancy that it took some time to figure the words out. I sat down and continued reading. "Of all the boys I have ever met and known I have to say that you are by far above all and forever the most SCURRILOUS!!!" The last word was written in big block letters. At the bottom of the page she had written, "Sealed with what I want to give you most, Ashley D." Underneath that she had drawn a big smiley face. Maybe the candy had given her the wrong idea.

I read that ending again, hoping Ashley wasn't going to be some kissy-face girl, but that's what the signature looked like.

I read the whole note again, stopping at the printed word *scurrilous*. I hated to admit that I didn't know what it meant. Probably had something to do with being smart and sophisticated and scurrying around helping people. That would describe me perfectly.

I went over to one of the big classroom dictionaries that we had been working with. That Ashley—she must have found a perfect word in the dictionary to describe me while she was doing the vocabulary work.

I flipped quickly through the pages.

. . . *scramble* . . . *scuffle* . . . *scupper* . . . *scurrilous*. There it was. I carefully read the definition: adj. —crude, vulgar, coarse.

I rubbed my eyes. Then I read it again. The same definition was still there. I was shocked. I was also mad at myself that I had wasted my lunch money on a girl. Never again!

I went back to my desk, got a paper and pencil, and started browsing quickly through the dictionary. There were some real zingers in there. Wait till Ashley got my answer to her note!

. . . *hoyden*—a wild and unruly girl . . . *inane*—silly . . . *odious*—nasty.

I had collected five of the most insulting words I could find when Mrs. Phister said, "Murphy, whatever are you doing? I've never seen anyone have such a good time looking through a dictionary."

She probably thought I was looking for dirty words.

"Just finishing up my assignment, Mrs. Phister. I'm smiling because I won't have anything left to do over the weekend."

As I hurried out of the room I heard Mrs. Phister say, "Murphy, I thought you wanted to clean your desk."

I looked back and saw my messy desk. "I'll have to do it Monday, Mrs. Phister. I forgot—my mom's expecting me home." And I rushed out.

The phone was ringing as I got in my front door. It was Iggy, but he was laughing so hard I could hardly hear what he was saying. I thought about hanging up on him when he said, "Your mouth must still be on fire. I told you the taste was guaranteed." And he started cracking up again.

"Iggy," I shouted into the phone. "Stop laughing and talk to me. What was in that candy? Iggy?"

He gasped and gulped. He sounded like he was rolling on the floor. "Pepper, Murphy. It was hot pepper candy. I got it at the joke store. I wasn't going to give it to you, Murphy. But I couldn't help myself. When you offered to pay, I got carried away. You kept begging."

As I hung up the phone, I said to myself, "That's what you get, Murphy Old Nerd. You've learned the hard way."

Never again would I ever get desperate over a girl—even one as cute as Ashley.

CHAPTER FIVE

Saturday morning—the longest, the laziest, the most wonderful morning of the week. It would have been perfect, except for Dad's eggs.

I got down to the kitchen real early so I could treat myself to some bagels or English muffins. Or even some leftover cake.

But Dad was already up, working away at the stove with his frying pan and spatula.

"Just in time, Murphy. I figured out a way to improve on yesterday's eggs."

He scooped some white stuff onto a plate and followed me over to the table. I figured they couldn't be any worse than yesterday's.

I was wrong.

They looked almost the same, except for a bunch of green specks and the real weird smell coming from them. I tried a little piece. It was like chewing on yesterday's socks.

"Dad, what did you do to them?"

"Just added a little flavor, Murphy. I knew yesterday's eggs tasted too mild, so I spiced them up. Garlic and parsley—a good shake of each—topped off with olives. And I cooked them longer so they wouldn't be too soft."

That accounted for the smell and the funny green flecks. And the rubbery taste.

I loved my father, but love goes only so far. When he went back to the stove to clean up, I dumped the eggs into Mom's fern and tried to mix them in with the dirt. Maybe they would make good fertilizer.

I brought the empty plate to Dad.

"That was quick," he said. "And I can see how much you enjoyed them."

I waited until he left. No one was around—my brothers were still in bed, Mom was downstairs doing laundry, and Dad was probably getting ready for his morning workout.

All my problems faded away as I planned my day. Cartoons—hours of them. Snacks—tons of them to make up for no breakfast. And a long afternoon of fooling around with my friends.

I had just settled into Dad's lounge chair and was getting into a "Super Heroes" cartoon when Dad came stomping into the family room, dressed in his workout clothes.

He took one look at me sitting almost upside down eating a chocolate bar and blew a fit. As a coach, Dad's on a constant fitness kick.

"Murphy," he started. "Time to get you on a full-

25

scale program. Healthy breakfasts aren't enough. I'm taking you with me for a jog. You can start by doing an easy half mile.''

"Aw, Dad." Sprawled in front of the television in my favorite chair, I was feeling much too comfortable to move. "Do I have to?"

"Murphy, you're at the age where you could let yourself get fat and lazy. It's ten o'clock on a Saturday morning, and you're not even dressed yet. You're going jogging.''

I hated jogging. I had tried it once before with him when it was my own idea, and it was boring. I would rather clean my room. "Mom says I've got to clean my room.''

He didn't budge. "Later. Right now we've got some muscles to firm up—yours. Kids nowadays are too soft— but not my sons.''

I looked at Dad standing in front of me from my upside-down position and tried to hide the half-eaten candy bar.

He's tall and lean and hard. He jogs at least five miles a day, works out on weights, and never eats more than he should. He drives the rest of us crazy.

He reached down, pinched me around the middle just to make his point, and I knew I was doomed. Nothing would satisfy him at this point short of my death on the high school jogging track.

"Go ahead, Dad. I'll get dressed and catch up with you.''

Fat chance of that one. "Hurry up, Murphy. I'll wait. You can run your two laps and then walk home while I finish up." I noticed that the muscles around his jaw-bones were starting to flex, so I started to hustle.

The high school track was right around the corner from our house, a convenience I didn't appreciate. "I'll walk a few laps to limber up, Dad," I suggested. "Then I'll put that half mile away without breaking a sweat."

A half mile. That didn't look so bad. Two times around the track. I was starting to feel cocky. After all, I was pretty good in gym in school and we ran once in a while. I never really pushed myself, but I could show Dad. Then I could get back to my TV, and maybe even a snack since I would be running off all those calories.

I started to walk, but Dad reached out his long arm and stopped me. "We have to stretch first. Stop stalling. Think you can make even half a lap?"

That annoyed me. What did Dad think I was, some fluff-ball? I'd have to show him a thing or two.

After we stretched, we started off on a slow jog. Too slow, to my way of thinking, so I sprinted ahead of Dad for a quarter of a lap, turned around, and ran backward, waiting for him to catch up. When he did, I ran a few circles around him. We had covered half a lap and I was really cooking. I knew I could dance my way through two laps.

"Murphy," Dad said in his "here-comes-a-lecture" voice. "You'd better conserve your energy. Burn yourself out on the first half lap and you'll never make the rest."

"Dad," I answered. "You're talking to the Murph. I'm really a great runner. You should see me in gym." And to prove my point, I circled him once more. Fleetfoot Murphy. With wings on my feet. I was waiting for Dad to comment on my athletic abilities, but he just smiled and kept to his slow, even pace.

I wasn't sure exactly what happened, but toward the end of the first lap I started to feel like someone had punched me in the gut. All of a sudden I started panting. My stomach ached. My eyes watered.

"Hey, Dad," I said, trying to keep the gasping noise out of my voice. "Maybe we should walk half a lap."

"No way, Murph. You've got to start building stamina, and you don't do it by walking." I knew what was coming next. I had heard him say it a hundred times to his ball players. I just didn't want to hear it, but I didn't have much choice.

"No gain without some pain, Murphy." And he said it again for emphasis. "No gain without some pain."

We had just started the second lap, but I thought I'd collapse.

"Dad," I gasped. I started to make my breath come in loud, raspy gulps so he'd maybe believe my situation was serious. "Dad. My chest hurts. I can't breathe." I didn't know if a kid could have a heart attack. I was hoping Dad might think it was possible.

"Murphy," he said. "Stop whining. It takes too much energy. Use it to run. Breathe through your ears if you have to. You can make it. It's only half a mile. And we only have half a lap to go."

Half a lap! He might as well have said ten miles. I looked up and saw the track stretching out like an interstate highway in front of me. It was like running in slow motion—someone had tied lead weights to each of my ankles. Sweat was running into my eyes, making them hurt. And I couldn't even plead with Dad because I couldn't even talk.

Just when I was ready to give up and go to the North Pole, where I was sure I could live like a fat and happy walrus and never be forced to run, I heard Dad say, "Just around this last corner, Murphy. There's the finish line for you."

I looked up. It was true. A few more steps and my agony and torture would be over.

As I chugged to a halt at the finish line, I fell down into the grass next to the track, gasping dramatically for air. But Dad pulled me to my feet. "You've got to walk a lap, Murphy. That's the mistake lots of people make. If you don't walk a cool-down lap, you'll get cramps for real." Guess he didn't believe the pain I was in.

Dad and I started to walk. I figured he'd start hollering at me and lecturing me about how out of shape I was. But he didn't. Instead, he slapped me on the back and said, "Nice job. I'm proud of you, Murphy."

That made me straighten up a little bit and walk a little prouder. I had done it.

"And another thing," he continued. "After a few weeks of running with me, you'll start to get into shape. Pretty soon you'll be up to a mile and it won't feel like anything."

My shoulders slumped. A mile won't feel like anything, he said? Fat chance. But I knew I couldn't get out of his "program." The two laps couldn't have taken us more than ten minutes, but it felt like hours.

When I got home, I knew I had to talk to someone.

29

Not Mom—she'd been agreeing with Dad lately. And not my nineteen-year-old brother, Tony—he spent most of his time finding ways to make my life miserable.

So I settled for Ken, my oldest brother. He's the one who's twenty-two. Next to my father, he's the best one to go to for advice.

He was in his room, reading a karate magazine. He was a black belt in karate, so he was also in extremely good shape. But he'd lived longer with Dad than any of us boys, and I needed help getting out of this jogging thing.

He looked up from his magazine as I plopped on his bed. "Murphy," he said. "God, you look awful. What happened? Did you lose a fight?"

"It's Dad," I said, fluffing up his pillow and starting to stretch out. "He's got me on a program. I had to jog two whole laps this morning."

He watched as I snuggled my head into his pillow.

"Hey, Murphy," he said. "You're sweating all over my bed. And you're dirty. Sit on the floor, kid, willya?"

What a great guy. I had just run my brains out and he was making me sit on his hard floor. I slid onto the floor.

"What are you now, Murphy, ten? eleven?" he asked.

"Yeah, something like that," I answered, annoyed. I was starting to regret my decision to discuss this with him. He couldn't even remember how old I was.

"I knew it," he said. And he stretched back on his chair, putting his hands behind his head. He got a real faraway look in his eyes.

Then he said, "Dad did the same thing to me. And to

Tony. Listen, Murphy. Dad takes a lot of pride in his family. Jogging is his way of keeping you close to him while you're growing up. Besides, it'll get you in shape."

He got up and flexed his muscles. Then he did a 360-degree spinning side kick, yelling a loud "aiyeee." His leg flew high over his head. Terrific! Just what I needed to make me feel like a total blob. My brother the karate acrobat.

I got up and slumped out of the room. "Thanks, Ken," I mumbled. "Hope I can do the same for you someday."

"Any time, kid," he said. "Feel free to come and talk over your problems any time."

CHAPTER SIX

I spent Saturday afternoon at Peter's, playing football, and when I got home I was starved. Mom was standing by the stove, stirring something in a pot.

"What's for dinner, Mom?" I was having visions of roast beef with mashed potatoes or ziti and meatballs, when she dished out a plate filled with franks and beans.

"Dad and I are eating out tonight. And I have a special surprise for you."

"Franks and beans are a special surprise?"

"No, silly. It's about later. I met a wonderful new family who just moved into town last month. They have a child your age. Dad and I are going out with them tonight and you're going to stay at their house for a while. We're sharing a baby-sitter."

I wrinkled up my nose at the word *baby*.

"I'd rather stay home, Mom. I'm old enough to stay by myself." I didn't feel like meeting some new kid.

"Sorry, Murphy. Your dad and I think you're still too

young to be left alone. Tony and Ken are both going out, so you definitely need a sitter. You'll have a great time. I think she goes to your school."

"She? Who? You don't mean I have to spend time with a girl I don't even know. That's not fair, Mom."

"I didn't say anything about 'fair,' Murphy. Mr. and Mrs. Douglas were nice enough to invite us to the theater with them. It's for the Westford Shakespeare Festival for tonight and tomorrow afternoon. We're sharing the expense of the sitter, and they were kind enough to offer their house. You'll love Ashley—she's an adorable little girl."

I was so shocked I couldn't even talk. It seemed to be a good five minutes before I could get my lips and voice to work together.

I didn't dare tell Mom about all the trouble I was having with Ashley. She'd just blame me. I had to think of a way out of this.

"Mom, don't leave me with a girl. What will we talk about—dolls? Cooking? Blow-drying my hair?"

She just looked as if she didn't hear me.

I tried again, this time stepping right in front of her. "Leave me with Tony—I'll even pay him out of my allowance. You'll save money. P-l-e-a-s-e!" Not that I wanted to spend an evening alone with my nineteen-year-old brother, but anything would be better than Ashley.

"Oh, no you don't, kiddo," hollered Tony from the bathroom. His big old ears were like radar—especially when it meant doing me a favor. "I've got a big date tonight with Corinda, and I ain't sittin' for no baby."

He was always going out with creepy girls with creepy names. Not that I ever saw them, but I heard their mushy voices when I answered the phone, which was always for Tony lately. The first time Corinda called, she asked me how old I was, and before I could even answer started telling me how cute I must be and didn't I want to grow up to be as handsome as Tony. Yuck—creepy!

But I was desperate. I ran up to the bathroom. Tony was almost finished shaving—running his hand over his cheek while he pulled it to one side all lopsided.

"Tony," I pleaded. "Save me. You can bring Corinda here. I'll get lost—honest—you'll be all alone with Corinda. I'll even pay you. Anything." I was practically on my knees.

He stopped admiring himself, looked me in the eye, and said, "How much?"

"How much what?" I sometimes forget to listen to what I'm saying when I'm desperate.

"Money," he said flatly. A cold look came into his eye. "How much you got, Murphy?"

I had to think hard before answering. I might have been desperate, but I wasn't stupid.

Now, I am by nature a saver of money. I think I still have the first dollar anyone sent me in a birthday card. Not that I don't spend money—but I always manage to make sure it's Mom's or Dad's, not mine.

I looked into Tony's greedy eyes. "Five big bucks," I said, trying to make it sound like a fortune.

He never even answered me—just went back to stroking his cheeks.

"Okay. Ten. But that's the easiest ten bucks you'll ever make. And you get a good, cheap date with creepy old Corinda on top of it."

I knew I had him convinced. Trouble was—Dad wasn't.

"Forget it, Tony," Dad said, sucking in his cheeks and looking very stern. Dad could always manage to pop up at the wrong time. "*Once* I left you and Murphy home alone. *Once*. I trusted you two *once*. And only *once*." Dad had a way of repeating himself when he started to get really mad—and I could tell he was starting to steam, thinking about the one time Tony baby-sat for me.

"The two of you spent the evening like two savages—two barbarians living in a cave. It took me days to clean up. And I still can't figure out what that stink was . . . and that gooey mess in the kitchen."

I grabbed Dad quickly by the sleeve and started leading him away from the bathroom door. "C'mon, Dad," I said, my face starting to flush. "I can't wait to meet Ashley. Honest."

Anything to keep him from remembering the dinner Tony and I had tried to cook. I thought spaghetti would be a snap to make. Except that the sauce ended up splattered all over the kitchen because we forgot it was on the stove and it bubbled and boiled all over everything. And the spaghetti we tried to cook had turned into one big gigantic sticky glob.

So we had settled for peanut butter and jelly. Then we started a long game of tackle football in the family room, which meant pushing all the furniture out of the way. We figured we had plenty of time to clean up the kitchen and the family room, but of course we figured wrong.

When Mom and Dad came home, he yelled at us for almost an hour. Mom was just in shock. And for almost a week after that, every time Dad went into the kitchen, he stuck his fingers into another glob of spaghetti sauce or peanut butter. And then he'd start to yell all over again.

Tony stuck his head out of the bathroom door as we left. "Careful, bro," he laughed. "Don't let Ashley talk you into dancing. You have enough trouble walking straight without looking like a klutz." He was really enjoying himself.

For once I didn't even bother to argue with him. I started to worry about what Dad would do to me when we got to the Douglases and he found out that I had dumped Ashley's braid in paste and then tried to poison her with candy.

He hadn't spanked me in a long time, but I probably wouldn't sit down for a month. I only hoped he wouldn't do it in front of Ashley.

I broke out in an A-1 panic attack. "Mom," I tried. "I have a fever."

She felt my forehead and laughed. "Murphy, what's the matter? Getting nervous over a girl? Are you getting into that age? Do you have a crush on Ashley? I hear she's awfully pretty."

"Never mind, Mom. Let's go."

CHAPTER SEVEN

"**S**o you're Murphy. We've heard quite a bit about you." I peeked out from where I was hiding behind Dad. He tried to step to the side, but I stayed right behind him.

Mr. Douglas was watching me, nodding his head up and down. Suddenly, as he stuck out his hand, Dad reached behind him and shoved me out in front.

Before I knew what I was doing, I stuck my sweaty hand into Mr. Douglas's. "Ashley tells me you're in the gifted group with her."

I stood there with my eyes glued to the floor, waiting for the rest. Come on, Mr. Douglas, get it over with.

Dad kept poking me in the back, clearing his throat. He finally said, "Speak up, Murphy. Mr. Douglas is talking to you."

When I looked up at Mr. Douglas, I saw him smiling. Mrs. Douglas came in, looked at me, and said, "So this is Murphy. It's so nice to meet you." And she shook my hand, too. What was going on? Surely they didn't plan to leave me with Ashley, not after everything that happened.

But they did. As they walked out the door, Mrs. Douglas said, "Ashley's in the family room. Just walk straight through the kitchen, Murphy. And help yourself to anything you want to eat."

Dad gave me a stern look. "No junk, Murphy. Remember. You're on a program."

"Yeah, Dad. I remember."

I walked slowly through the kitchen and grabbed a brownie off a plate. I felt like I had landed on Mars or lost my memory or something. But if I had to face Ashley, it was going to be on a full stomach.

I stood in the doorway chewing on the brownie. Ashley was watching TV. She was dressed in a pair of old jeans and a baggy blue shirt that looked like it belonged to her father. Maybe she didn't know I was coming—she sure wasn't dressed for company.

When she saw me, she turned off the TV, walked over to me, and just stood in front of me. I figured she'd smack me, but I didn't even put up my hands. I deserved whatever she did.

"Hi, Murphy. Want to watch TV?" Now I knew I was crazy.

I couldn't stand it. "Ashley. Look. About your braid. I'm really sorry. And that candy . . ." The words started to tumble out. "I didn't know—"

She cut me off. "Yeah, I know you didn't."

"Huh? You knew? What do you mean, you knew? What did you know?"

"About Iggy and his pepper candy. Steffie Whiffet told me. She was with me when I took a bite, and I was so mad at you. That's why I wrote you that note."

"How did Steffie know? And when did she tell you?" This wasn't happening. I started to pinch myself to see if I was dreaming.

"Steffie's always hanging around. She's a real pest. But I let her do favors for me. Anyway, after school she told me that she heard that Iggy gave you that candy. And that you didn't know. I didn't know whether to believe her—Steffie's not too bright, you know. But then I figured if you had enough nerve to show up here tonight, maybe it was true. So I'm sorry about the note. Truce?"

And she stuck her hand out to shake mine. I quickly rubbed my hand on my pants. I didn't want it to be all damp and sticky. When we shook hands, it felt nice. She had a strong handshake for a girl—not all floppy and silly. Maybe this wasn't going to be such a bad night after all.

The baby-sitter was doing homework, and Ashley and I spent the time talking about sports. It turned out we both liked basketball and baseball best of all. We tied 5–5 in ten games of checkers, and even though she beat me in a game of Go to the Head of the Class (and only because I got some bad breaks with the luck cards), we ended up figuring we were two of the smartest kids in Westford.

The time went by so fast, I was sorry I had to leave.

"Bye, Ashley, and thank you so much for having me over, Mr. and Mrs. Douglas," I said in my most polite voice. "See you tomorrow, Ashley." Mom and Dad exchanged odd looks; there was, after all, a big change in my attitude, but I think they were proud of me.

I couldn't stop talking about Ashley all the way home. Dad winked at Mom and Mom just kept saying "um-hmmm" in that "told you so" voice.

I didn't want them to get the wrong idea, so I said, "She's really different, you know. Not like a real girl. She doesn't act all squishy and stupid like most of them do. It's almost like she's really not a girl."

CHAPTER EIGHT

"**I** told you. She's *not* my girlfriend." It was Sunday afternoon. I had just showered after my half-mile jog with Dad, and I was combing my hair in the bathroom when Tony walked in. Then Kenny walked in behind him. With two brothers like them, I didn't get much privacy.

"Then what are you showering and combing your hair for?" Kenny asked.

"You spent last night with her and now you're going over there again. Sounds serious to me," Tony said, reaching over and mussing up my hair.

"Hey. Cut that out. I only showered because I was all sweaty from jogging." I was getting mad. Mom and Dad were waiting to leave for the Douglas's and I just wanted to make sure I looked okay. "Besides, she's not like that. We're just friends. Not like those creeps Tony hangs around with. And get out of the bathroom. The door was closed when you just barged in, you know."

"You're really growing up, little brother," Tony said. "Next thing I know you'll be wanting my car keys!" They both slapped me on my butt and walked out, laughing hysterically. What a pair of comedians! I combed my hair again.

I grabbed a bag of baseball cards, figuring Ashley and I could sort through them, and ran out to the car. I knew Ashley would like helping me because we had become friends. And she was definitely not a typical weird girl.

At least that's what I thought. But it seemed like Ashley had all the personalities of a Jekyll and Hyde. Last night the good Dr. Jekyll; today the crazy Ms. Hyde.

I could sense that something was different as soon as I walked in the door. She greeted me with this real soft voice, "Oh, hello, Murphy. It's so-o-o-o nice to see you again." Then she did something real dumb. She turned her back to me, peeked over one shoulder, and gave me a little finger wave and a silly smile.

I couldn't believe what I was seeing. I looked for the door, figuring I'd better get out of there, but Mom and Dad had already left with the Douglases. I cleared my throat. Ashley was still posing. "Ashley, what's the matter? You sick or something?"

She turned around slowly, tilted her head to one side, fluffed her hair, and giggled. "Oh, Murphy. You look so nice today." And then she just stood there like she expected me to pay her a compliment. So I did.

"Ashley. Where'd you get that dumb-looking outfit?" She was wearing some kind of pink tights, patent leather shoes, and a short, twirly skirt. "You trying to look like a cheerleader?"

She wasn't amused. In fact, she looked pretty annoyed. She stood up bone straight, flattened down her skirt with one hand and her hair with the other, and said, "I didn't have time to change after dance class. I take tap and ballet."

My mouth opened before I had time to think. "I didn't know baby elephants could dance." I was sorry I had said it, right as soon as the words were out of my mouth. This was not going to be a great afternoon.

She glared at me. I thought she was going to try to punch me, but just then the baby-sitter walked in from the kitchen. "Hi, guys," she said. "Getting ready for another great time?"

By this time Ashley was so mad she could hardly talk. "I don't think so," she snarled. "Considering the fact that I beat Murphy at Go to the Head of the Class last time and had to let him win a few games of checkers so he wouldn't feel as stupid as he really is."

That did it. "Stupid?" I hollered. "You're calling me stupid? Name the game. I'll beat you at anything you name. I did you a favor last time. I could have creamed you, but you're new in town. I just didn't want to embarrass you."

She looked straight at me and clenched her fists down by her side. "Don't worry about it, Murphy. I'm not easily embarrassed by *little* boys. I'm obviously more mature than you'll ever be." She had started talking real slow and put on this real phony, sophisticated voice. "I'll challenge you at anything," she continued. "How about math? or science? How about even dressing in fashion? You obviously know nothing about that."

I was so mad, my voice almost squeaked. "How about karate, Ashley? How about my foot up the side of your head?"

"Now, children," the sitter was saying. "It's important to get along." But I could tell she was on Ashley's side from the way she was standing next to her. "How about a contest that you're both good at. How about a reading contest?"

I could hardly believe my ears. Now, I just happen to be the best reader in the class. I know that because I got a reading award at the end of the last four years.

I started to smile. Then I saw Ashley smiling, too. "Good idea," she said. "But I have to warn you, Murphy. The reason I was selected for the gifted group was because I was the very best in all my subjects last year."

"Oh, yeah?" I laughed. "Where did you go to school— Dumbo Elementary School?"

She didn't answer, just gave me another of her dirty looks designed to melt iron. But I was getting very used to them. And I was starting to realize that I had made a big mistake thinking Ashley and I could ever be friends.

She picked up the *Westford Times*. "You go first," she said. "If you can read at all."

Of course I could read. And I did a great job on an article about our mayor dedicating a new park.

Ashley's turn. She started to read the same article, but I just laughed. "Big deal, Ashley. Can't be original? Can't read unless you've heard it before?"

44

"You didn't clarify the rules, Murphy," she said in a snotty voice. "But I guess that's to be expected."

"Most people with any brains could figure out the rules by themselves," I replied.

The baby-sitter interrupted. "Now, kids. Let's be nice. After all, we just want to have some fun."

Yeah, some fun!

Ashley picked out another article and read it through. She stumbled over a few words, but she made a big point to read with a lot of feeling. Only someone like Ashley could read a newspaper article with that much drama. But I guess she did okay, even though I knew my article was really harder.

When she was done, she put down the paper dramatically, turned to the sitter, and said, "You be the judge." She said it like she thought she had definitely gotten the better of me.

The sitter looked first at me and then turned slowly to Ashley. "I declare the winner is . . . both of you," she announced finally. "You're both wonderful readers. Really. I'm so impressed with both of you. And Ashley, I should add that you read with great expression."

Oh, brother! What a joke. I could read circles around Ashley and we both knew it. Expression still couldn't make up for mistakes, even though girls always acted like it could.

But I was tired—of Ashley, of the sitter, of these ridiculous games, of being with girls. I went over to the TV, turned on a soccer game, and sat glued to the set until Mom and Dad finally showed up. It took me all of thirty seconds to get my jacket on and get out the door. I waited in the car while they said their good-byes.

"Murphy," Mom said when she got in the car. "I've never known you to be in such a hurry or to be so rude. What happened?"

"Nothing, Ma." I didn't want to talk about it. "But I've had enough of Ashley Douglas to last me a lifetime. If you put us together again in the same room, I'm not making any promises about my behavior."

I slumped down in the backseat, totally disgusted.

"I can't understand it," Mom was saying to Dad. "Nora Douglas was telling us how excited Ashley was over Murphy's visit. She even wore her new outfit and made her mother blow-dry her hair. She said that Ashley had kind of a crush on Murphy. What could have happened?"

Oh, brother. Why did things have to be so complicated? Yesterday we were almost friends. Today we did nothing but fight and Mom had the nerve to suggest Ashley had a crush on me. *Yuck*!

CHAPTER NINE

It was war. And my way of dealing with Ashley was to try to ignore her—completely. There was only one problem. Ashley started being a pest again. Throughout the whole next week she was like a mosquito buzzing around my ear. She seemed to be out of her seat every two minutes—to sharpen her pencil, get extra paper, go to the bathroom. And every time she did, she'd pull my hair, twerp me in the head with her fingers, or whisper something sarcastic.

Every recess she'd hang around Peter and me. And there was Steffie, hanging right behind her. And whatever Ashley wanted, Steffie ran and did it.

"Come on, Peter," I finally said one morning before school started when I couldn't shake Ashley. "I've got to go to the boys' room."

When we were alone, I asked Peter, "What am I going to do? That girl is trying to drive me nuts. I know she hates me, but this is ridiculous."

Peter laughed. "I don't think she hates you. I think Ashley really likes you."

"Now *you're* trying to drive me nuts. Ashley? *Likes* me? Give it a break. She just likes to bug me."

"I know," he answered. "That's part of the game girls play. Besides, she's not bad looking."

"Yeah. But looks aren't everything. Come on. We're going to be late."

When we got to class, Mrs. Phister was nowhere in sight. Iggy Sands, who couldn't be left alone for five seconds, was rolling up little balls of paper and bouncing them off the heads of everyone around him. I was impressed by how good his aim was until I got hit. Naturally I had to fire a ball back at him.

But I missed Iggy and hit Steffie by mistake. She didn't say anything, but suddenly Ashley became Steffie's big defender. "Murphy, that was really mean," she hollered.

She must have realized she'd never be able to hit me with a little ball. So she wadded up a big sheet of paper, stood up quickly, and beaned me right in the forehead. In a matter of seconds the whole room was out of control. Naturally Mrs. Phister walked in. She looked surprised until a big ball bopped her off the side of her head. Then she looked mad.

We all sat at attention as she looked around, trying to figure out who to blame.

"Girls and boys," she said finally. "I have just come from a meeting and have an announcement to make. Dr. Harder has officially declared the month of October *Cooperation Month*. Each classroom is expected to come

48

up with projects that will encourage the spirit of cooperation."

She paused, and started looking straight at me. I realized then that I was still holding the paper ball that Ashley had clonked me in the head with. I quickly shoved it into my desk.

"Now listen carefully while I explain to all of you what our class is going to do." She adjusted her glasses on her nose and swatted back a few strands of hair that had fallen in her face.

"We are going to hold a contest. We will call it 'Catch a Kid Cooperating.' And there will be a big prize for the most cooperative student at the end of the month."

Contest and *prize* were like magic words. Suddenly we were all a little more interested.

Mrs. Phister went to her desk and got sheets of light brown construction paper and scissors. "Each of you will make an ice-cream cone out of these sheets of paper. Just the cone. Cut one out and decorate it with your name. Then we'll put all of the cones along the bottom of the big bulletin board in the back of the room."

I swiveled around in my chair. The bulletin board stretched along the whole back wall. It was empty except for plain yellow paper and a big sign that was printed across the top: CATCH A KID. SCOOPS FOR COOPERATION.

Pretty corny, I thought. But teachers will try anything to get kids to be good.

Mrs. Phister was passing out the paper and scissors. "Every time you're caught being cooperative—helping

in some way or being considerate to someone else—
you'll get a scoop of ice cream with your name on it to
put on top of your cone."

Most of the kids in class were getting pretty excited
about the whole thing. Except Raymond Stubbs. It always took Raymond longer than anybody to catch on to
everything. He raised his hand slowly and, looking very
puzzled, asked, "But, Mrs. Phister, won't the ice cream
melt?"

Poor Raymond. Some of the girls started to giggle and
a couple of the guys groaned. Iggy Sands, who sat
behind Raymond, stood up, put his fingers in his ears,
crossed his eyes, and swayed from side to side, making
everyone laugh. I just looked down at the floor. I hated
when they made fun of him. He was really great at "ups
and downs"—smacking a rubber ball that was attached
to a paddle with a long elastic. I once saw him hit the
ball 137 times in a row. You've got to respect someone who can do that, even if they're not so great in
class.

A loud clearing of the throat from Mrs. Phister along
with a very stern look made the kids quiet down. Iggy
sat down sheepishly.

"No, Raymond," she explained patiently. "The scoops
are made of paper, just like the cones are. When you do
something nice for someone, I'll give you one to pin
up."

Then she looked around at the rest of us. "But it
wouldn't surprise me, with the attitude I see today, if no
one wins the contest."

Ashley had the next question. "What's the prize,

Mrs. Phister?'' Ashley was probably trying to decide whether she should even bother. Being nice wasn't something that came naturally to Ashley.

"That's a good question, Ashley." Mrs. Phister started smiling like she was about to offer us a million bucks or something. "The prize, boys and girls, will be . . ." and she paused like she expected to hear a drumroll or something. Like I said, corny. ". . . the prize will be a superscooper triple scoop ice-cream sundae for the winner and three friends at the best ice-cream shop in town—The Sundae School."

Teachers somehow have a way of making little things sound like a big deal. Oh well, I figured a contest is a contest, and I'm always up for a challenge.

We all started snipping away at our cones and bunching up in little groups, talking about our favorite flavors of ice cream. Ashley and Jennifer and Deanna were making a big production out of it. They'd take a few snips or do a little coloring, and then stop and hold it up so that everyone could admire their work. Steffie kept trying to get involved with them, but they all kind of ignored her. So she just worked near them and pretended she was part of their group.

I finished doing my cone in no time. Nothing fancy, just a neat brown cone with my name in block letters.

Then I noticed Raymond just sitting there at his desk—all alone—not doing anything. I walked over and stood in front of him. "Hey, Raymond," I said. "How come you're not cutting out your cone?"

He looked down at the paper and scissors on his

desk. "Aw, Murphy," he said, looking a little like he wanted to cry. "I'm no good at making stuff, and I won't win any scoops anyway."

I hated it when someone like Raymond looked sad. "Sure you will," I said, making my voice sound extra cheerful. "You're good at helping—you're always doing jobs for Mrs. Phister. I'll bet you're one of the most helpful kids she has." Raymond was also the biggest kid she had, so he was always asked to move stuff or carry stuff. I figured Raymond was a few years older than the rest of us. That's what made me feel even sadder for him.

He looked up and smiled at me just a little. "You think so, Murphy? You're not just saying that, are you?"

"Would I kid a friend?"

"But I don't know how to start. My cone'll come out all crooked."

I looked around. Mrs. Phister was busy at her desk in front of the room. I made sure I was standing between her and Raymond so she couldn't see what I was doing if she looked up.

"C'mon, Raymond," I whispered. "I'll do it for you. Just keep an eye on Mrs. Phister so she doesn't see what we're doing." Mrs. Phister was kind of a bug about doing your own work. She was always blowing her top if she caught any of us copying.

I started making Raymond's cone. I was trying to hurry, but I didn't want to mess it up. I guess I wanted Raymond to be proud of it, so I made a pretty complicated cone with dips and points—not just a plain old triangle.

I was practically making the last snip when I felt someone standing behind me—someone tall—someone watching every move I was making. I didn't even have to look. Raymond had been so interested watching me cut out his cone that he didn't see Mrs. Phister come up behind me.

Raymond looked sad again. "Sorry, Murphy," he said quietly. "I forgot to watch."

I quickly put the paper and scissors down, hoping she wouldn't guess what I was up to.

Mrs. Phister put a hand on my shoulder. "Murphy. What *are* you doing? Bothering Raymond?" She was very protective of kids like Raymond and didn't like it when kids made fun of him.

"No, I, uh, uh, I was just . . . uh . . . Raymond couldn't . . . uh . . ." I didn't know what to say. I didn't want to get Raymond in trouble for not doing his own work. But I didn't want to get in trouble either.

All of a sudden, Raymond spoke up—louder and clearer than I'd ever heard him. "It's my fault, Mrs. Phister. I didn't know how to do it. Murphy just came over to help me. Murphy doesn't bother me. Honest."

Mrs. Phister looked at me, then at Raymond, then at the cone on his desk. She turned around quickly, and without a word, walked to her desk, fiddled around with something, and then came back. I felt like I was glued to the floor.

"Class," she said real loud. "I'd like your attention."

Here it comes, I thought. Public humiliation. Whenever she caught one of us in a "bad act," as she called it, she'd announce it to the whole class. She told us once that criminals in New England in the 1600s were put on display in the middle of town for everyone to see. That was called a *deterrent*. People would try to be good so they wouldn't be humiliated in public. Mrs. Phister often ran her classroom that way. She was big on *deterrents*.

Everyone had stopped what they were doing. We all enjoyed someone else's trouble and were willing to pay attention when someone got punished. It was so quiet I could hear the person next to me breathing.

She put a hand on my shoulder. I looked at Raymond for help, but he was looking away. "I would like all of you to look at Murphy," she said very seriously. "Because he took the time and the trouble to help a classmate on this project, I am proud to present him with the very first scoop of the contest."

I was shocked. I could hardly believe what I was hearing. Was it possible? But there it was. Mrs. Phister was handing me a pink cut-out ice-cream scoop with my name on it. I looked at the big smile on her face. Then I looked proudly around the room.

Funny—no one seemed to be much interested anymore, except a couple of my friends, who came over to look at the scoop. I guess that's typical. When there's trouble, everyone watches. When someone gets praised, no one much cares. But I felt pretty good. This contest was going to be easy. I could almost taste that ice cream already.

When I went to pin my cone and my scoop on the

board, my cone ended up next to Ashley's. She came up next to me and said real snotty, "Think you're a pretty big deal, huh, Murphy? That's probably the only scoop you'll get. I'm glad my cone is next to yours. That way, when my scoops hit the ceiling, you'll understand what greatness really is. And believe me, that's the closest you'll come to it."

That Ashley. She must have been taking lessons in how to be snotty. And to think I used to like her. But even she wasn't going to make me lose my cool. Not now. I was feeling too good to let her upset me.

But I felt her challenge and I knew that I had to beat her. It didn't matter if I won the contest, but I had to stay ahead of Ashley.

CHAPTER TEN

"**D**id you see that? Did you see how she just handed me that scoop? And it was the first one!"

I was having a great time on the way home, bragging to Peter and Greg and Michael about my scoop. They kept trying to change the subject, but I kept talking about how I would probably win the contest.

I was feeling pretty terrific until Peter looked at me strangely and said, "Hey, Murphy. Where's your book bag?"

I stopped dead in my tracks. I felt around my back to where my backpack should have been. No wonder I was feeling so light. "Oh, no. I must've left it in school."

Greg shook his head very seriously. "Too bad, Murphy. And Mrs. Phister sure piled on the homework for tonight."

"That's the way it goes," added Michael. "A scoop today—a zero tomorrow." And they all started to laugh.

56

I hated to forget homework, because Mrs. Phister always made such a fuss. She had a chart hanging in the room for homework. Anyone who didn't have homework done got a big fat zero for the day next to his name. It happened to me once during the first week of school, and she made a big public announcement to the class. "Zero for today, Murphy." Then, as she slowly and carefully drew the big circle next to my name, she said it again to make sure everyone heard. "Murphy Darinzo. Z-E-E-R-O-O-O." Talk about embarrassment.

Well, I couldn't let that happen again. Not after getting the first scoop.

"Hey, guys," I said. "Walk back to school with me, willya?" We were all standing by Peter's front door.

"No way, Murphy," said Peter. "Once I'm home, that's it."

Michael slapped me on the back and said, "See ya later."

Greg waved a big good-bye.

I turned around and started the long walk back to school. Peter called after me, "But I'll see you for breakfast, Murphy."

I couldn't get mad at him. He'd been feeding me every morning, ever since Dad had started to cook for me.

No one was around as I walked down the hall to my classroom. Everything was so quiet and empty. I found my book bag under my desk. Then I went to the back of the room to admire my scoop. Everybody's cone had been hung up and they all looked empty—except mine, of course.

As I looked around the rest of the room, I was shocked to see that the big blackboard in front of the room hadn't been erased. Mrs. Phister liked things neat and tidy, so she elected a monitor every week to make sure the room was shipshape at the end of the day. The monitor did things like make sure all books were put away, there were no stray papers on the floor, the plants were watered, and the blackboard was erased. This week's monitor was Ashley.

But here it was, after three o'clock, no Ashley in sight, and the board was totally covered with words and problems. "Murphy," I said to myself out loud (I like to talk to myself when I know there's nobody around). "Will you look at that! It will serve Ashley right to get in trouble." I started to leave.

I stopped and mumbled, "But then again, this could mean another scoop for you." I stood there thinking. Then I made a decision. "Time to rack up another scoop, Murphy. Get busy, boy." (I was sounding like my father.) "Clean that board until it shines."

It felt like it took forever to get the board perfect. I put a lot of effort into that job. I even pulled over a chair to make sure I could reach up to the very top.

When I thought I was finished, I stepped back to admire my work. One corner was still looking smudgy, so I put an extra few minutes into it.

What a job. My arm was hurting because I had worked so hard to polish the board. But it was worth the effort. That board was black and shining by the time I was done. It almost looked washed. Actually, if I could have gotten my hands on a bucket of water and a sponge, I would have done that, too. When I'm into something, I'm into it. I really get carried away.

Feeling extra proud and certain of earning scoop number two (before Ashley had even started), I slipped my book bag onto my back and headed home. I had this contest won. I was already planning my big day with my friends at The Sundae School, and that didn't include Ashley. What a great day! What a great life!

CHAPTER ELEVEN

I was so excited about getting to school that I got up extra early the next morning. Only Mom was in the kitchen.

As I reached for the cereal bowl and cereal, I said, "I'm gonna have a quick bowl of cereal for breakfast. Dad's still asleep and I don't want to bother him with my breakfast."

"I don't know, Murphy," said Mom. "You know how much he enjoys making breakfast for you. He's proud of you for sticking to your program."

"I know, Mom. But just this one morning won't matter. And like I said, I don't want to bother Dad."

"Did I hear someone mention my name?" I heard a deep voice behind me. Dad had to be the world's fastest dresser. "No need to bother with the cereal, Murphy. I'll have breakfast for you in a jiffy. I have a special treat for you this morning, and you're going to love it."

"Right, Dad," I said, trying to put some enthusiasm into my voice. After all, when a parent puts that much effort into a project, it's hard to tell him it's not as great as he thinks it is.

Mom gave me a hug and said, "Enjoy breakfast, Murphy. I'm leaving early for school." And she winked at me and left.

I sat at the table, waiting for my surprise, letting my mind drift over the great day I had ahead. No little thing like breakfast could even begin to spoil it.

"How do you like this?" Dad asked as he proudly placed a dish in front of me.

It took a while for me to figure out what, exactly, he had done. I looked into one large round white blob, like a big flat white pancake. But there were brown spots melted into it.

I kept looking between Dad and the plate, hoping to get a clue.

"So? What do you think?" he asked expectantly.

"Dad," I said, trying to think of something to say. "I don't know what to say."

He started to look serious. "I know what you're thinking, Murphy. I know I'm against your eating candy. But you've been so good, and I didn't know how else to make a smiley face. So I used M&Ms."

I looked closer at my plate. So that's what it was. Flat egg white with M&Ms cooked into it. It did kind of look like a face, even though the eyes and nose were all kind of melty and squishy.

"Fascinating, Dad. Thanks."

He patted me on the back. "I want to make sure Tony and Ken are up. I'll be back in a few minutes if you want more."

As Dad went upstairs, Tony came into the kitchen, took one look at my plate, and said, "I see Dad's still cooking for you, Murphy. How much longer do you think it's going to last?"

"Forever," I said. "Until I'm dead."

"Keep eating that stuff, and you might not have to wait too long."

I watched Tony make himself some toast. As he started to sit down, he looked again into my plate, got up, and walked into the front hall. When he came back, he was dragging my book bag and, stopping for a minute, grabbed something out of a cabinet and sat down.

"Tony," I said, annoyed. "What are you doing with my book bag?" I watched as he tucked it between us, unzipped it, and shoved something into it.

"Shhhh," he whispered. "Quick. The eggs. In here."

It took me a minute to figure out what he was doing. I looked into my book bag and saw a plastic food bag propped open.

He punched me in the leg. "Hurry up. What are you waiting for? Before Dad comes back. *Now!*" I held my plate over the book bag while he quickly scraped the eggs into the plastic bag. I wanted to tell him to be careful not to spill any, but I didn't want to push my luck.

He also dropped his own two pieces of peanut butter toast into another plastic bag and stuffed them in between my books. "Just so you won't starve," he whispered. Just as Dad was coming back into the kitchen, he knotted the plastic bags and zipped up my book bag.

Dad looked pleased when he saw the clean plate. "How were they, Murphy?"

"Better than ever, Dad." And I winked at Tony.

"That good, huh? But don't get used to the candy treat—that was just for today."

"Don't worry, Dad. I promise I won't get used to them."

When I got to Peter's house, Mrs. Patterson had a place set for me. This kind woman was feeding me breakfast every morning—no questions asked. As she started to put some toast into the toaster, I said, "Thanks, anyway, Mrs. Patterson. But I brought my own this morning."

She looked at me oddly as I unzipped my book bag and pulled out the toast. A little scrunched and crumby, but after what Tony had done for me, I planned to eat every bite.

I spotted the other plastic bag and pulled it out. "Okay if I use your garbage, Mrs. Patterson?" I asked, holding the bag of eggs.

She looked startled. "Murphy! What in heaven's name is that mess?"

I knew she probably didn't want it in her garbage. Mrs. Patterson is a very clean person. But I couldn't keep carrying the eggs in my book bag. "It was supposed to be a science experiment for school. But it got smooshed together in my bag."

As I was holding it over the garbage, Peter came over for a close look. "So that's what you've been telling me about," he said. "I wouldn't have believed it."

When we got to school, I left Peter standing outside talking to the guys while I hurried into class. I was the first one in the room, so I double-checked two things—my scoop (it was still the only one there) and my blackboard (when you work hard on something, you start to get a feeling of ownership, even for a blackboard). I walked up to the board and wiped off the chalk tray underneath it with my shirt-sleeve. I was wearing a black long-sleeved shirt and it got kind of covered with dust. I knew Mom wouldn't approve, but a job is a job.

I couldn't wait for school to start. Mrs. Phister would come into the room and say, "How nice the board looks."

Then Ashley would have to admit she forgot. And if she didn't, I'd remind her.

Then Mrs. Phister would say, "My. I wonder who the wonderful person was who did such an outstanding job on the board. You'll have to thank him, Ashley." That would be my cue to modestly raise my hand.

"Oh, Murphy," she'd say, smiling sweeter than ever. "I should have known. You are my star student. You are the most cooperative student. Here's a scoop, Murphy. We should probably stop the contest now."

Ashley would have to thank me and agree with Mrs. Phister. Then I'd raise my hand to stop them because I really am a very modest and humble person. Really. "Let's give them a chance, Mrs. Phister," I'd say.

I was so busy in my daydream that I hardly realized that the rest of the class and Mrs. Phister had come in. As we did the pledge to the flag, I noticed Mrs. Phister kept looking at the board. Pretty soon, Murphy, I kept thinking.

When we sat down, Mrs. Phister stood in front of the room, tapping her toe on the floor. She was very quiet. "Ashley," she said finally. "You are usually such a good class monitor. I told you *not* to erase the board last night. I told you distinctly that I wanted to continue to work with the same lesson. Didn't you remember?"

I couldn't believe what I was hearing. I looked down so she wouldn't see my shocked face, and then I noticed the chalk dust on my sleeve. A dead giveaway. I quickly moved my arm onto my lap and slumped down in my seat.

Ashley was saying, "I didn't, Mrs. Phister. Honest. Someone must have done it after I left. Someone who wanted to get me into trouble." She was so upset, I thought she might cry.

I knew what I should have done. I should have gotten her off the hook. I should have stood right up and admitted my guilt. I should have acted like a man. I should have left for Alaska last night.

But I didn't do any of those things. I just sat there like I was nailed to my chair, my hair feeling all prickly on top of my head, my cheeks burning with guilt—a typical panic attack. Murphy, Murphy, I thought. You are going to get caught. Any second now.

But I didn't. Mrs. Phister controlled her anger as best she could. "It's okay, Ashley," she said, barely moving her lips. "I'm sure there's a reasonable explanation." Then she added quietly, "I don't know what happened, but there must be an explanation."

As her anger calmed down, so did my panic attack. I was going to get away with this one. But I hadn't done anything wrong. And all that work for nothing. Murphy, I thought, you are one big dope. No ice cream and no contest is worth this kind of aggravation.

CHAPTER TWELVE

The rest of the morning was pretty boring. Ashley managed to pick up a scoop by being teacher's pet again to Mrs. Phister, and a couple of other kids got one, too, including Steffie Whiffet, who got one for doing something nice for Ashley. So now my scoop didn't look so special anymore. True glory doesn't last too long.

At lunch I was still feeling kind of depressed. I couldn't believe I did so much work and almost got in trouble for doing it. Life just wasn't fair sometimes. I didn't want to talk to anyone, so I sat by myself in a corner of the cafeteria, pulled out a piece of bubble gum, and started on a good, hard chew.

Raymond Stubbs must have seen me sitting by myself, so he came over and sat down beside me.

"Hey, Murph," he said. "What's the matter? You look like you lost your best friend."

"Nah. It's nothing, Raymond. I was just thinking

how good deeds aren't always what they're cracked up to be."

He looked at me, puzzled. "Huh?"

"Nothing. Forget it." I looked over at his sad-looking lunch box. Raymond was one of the few kids in class who still carried a lunch box to school. He had nothing in it but a couple of unpeeled carrots that were pretty wilted.

"Raymond," I said. "You on a diet or something?"

He shut his lunch box quickly. I guess he was embarrassed. "Mom didn't have much time this morning. So I just grabbed a couple of things out of the fridge. I like carrots."

"Here. Take my lunch. I haven't touched it and to tell you the truth I'm not really hungry. Here. Take my milk, too. I haven't opened it yet."

He looked at me curiously. "I can't take your lunch."

"Sure you can. I told you, I'm not hungry. No sense letting it go to waste." I shoved the bag and the milk toward him.

"Gee, thanks. That's really nice of you. This looks like a great lunch."

"It's nothing, Raymond. Hope you enjoy it." It really was nothing. I usually enjoyed lunch, but for once in my life I wasn't hungry. I was feeling so lousy and so stupid, I just couldn't eat. I packed my mouth with two more pieces of bubble gum and tried to lose myself in my chewing.

Just before the end of the day, Mrs. Phister said, "Murphy, I'd like to see you for a minute after school."

My heart sank down to my toes. I should have known I'd never get away with it.

I stood in front of her desk after everyone else had left except Ashley, who was erasing the board. Mrs. Phister looked up at me and said, "Murphy, I know what you did."

I knew it. Someone had seen me. Someone had squealed. Either that or she had figured it out from the chalk dust on my sleeve. I started rubbing at it.

I looked down. I could feel my cheeks getting hot again. Two panic attacks in one day was too much for anyone. "I don't know what to say, Mrs. Phister. I just thought—"

She cut me off. "It was very nice of you, Murphy. Raymond told me how you gave him your lunch. He appreciated it. He wanted me to know how nice you've been to him."

And two shocks in one day was more than I could handle. She was handing me a scoop.

"But I didn't do it for a scoop, Mrs. Phister. Honest. I don't deserve this." I put the scoop down on her desk. "I wasn't hungry at lunch. I would have thrown my lunch away."

She picked up the scoop and handed it back to me. "You certainly do deserve this. Giving your lunch to someone who didn't have one is truly in the spirit of cooperation. Now, hang up your scoop. I have a meeting to attend." She picked up some papers and left the room.

I got her stapler and pinned my second scoop on top

of the first one. I was in the lead once more. I stood there for a while, watching Ashley work on the board. Then I walked over, picked up an eraser, and started to help.

She looked at me and frowned. "Forget it, Murphy. I'm not telling Mrs. Phister you helped, so don't bother. It won't get you another scoop."

"I'm not doing it for a scoop. I'm just doing it to help. I think it was real mean of someone to erase the board last night. Maybe it was a mistake."

"No, it wasn't. I think someone was just trying to get me into trouble." But she didn't seem mad anymore. We didn't talk while we worked. When we were done, she said. "Thanks, Murphy. You can be pretty nice when you want."

"Yeah, well—thanks for the compliment, Ashley." And I started to leave.

"Murphy?"

"Yeah, Ashley?"

"I'm still going to beat you in the contest."

"Right, Ashley."

"But you know what, Murphy?"

"No. What, Ashley?"

"When I win, you'll be one of the people I take for ice cream."

"Don't do me any favors, Ashley."

I walked out of the room shaking my head and almost bumped into Steffie Whiffet, who was coming in.

"Steffie," I said, surprised to see her. "What are you doing here?"

"I was going to see if Ashley needed any help. She's monitor, you know."

"What do you want to hang around Ashley for?" I said, feeling annoyed. "All she does is use you."

She almost got mad. "She's very nice. She helps me with my homework sometimes. And I heard her say she's going to take you for ice cream if she wins. You should be nicer to her. She likes you, you know."

"Sure she does. Just about as much as I like the dentist."

CHAPTER THIRTEEN

"**D**ad, can I ask you something?" We were out jogging early on a Saturday morning a few weeks later. It was the middle of October and I had been on Dad's program for two weeks. It was still a pain to jog, but at least it was getting so that I could talk and run at the same time.

"Sure, Murphy. That's what I love about jogging with you. We get to have real man-to-man chats."

I ignored the comment. Dad could get a little corny sometimes. "Does it ever get easy?" I asked.

"Jogging? Well, not really. You'll get better at it, but I can't say it'll ever get easy."

"I don't mean jogging, Dad. I mean life. When does it get easy?"

He was quiet for a long time. "Life's a little like jogging, Murphy. You get better at it. But it doesn't ever get really easy." He started talking about how much harder it was when he was a kid, and I nodded a lot and grunted once in a while. But I kind of tuned out. Dad's a great father, but like most adults, he doesn't always understand.

At breakfast the conversation turned to my Halloween costume. Mom always made my costume and I had won the Best Costume prize for my grade for the last three years at Westford Elementary. I was hoping for four.

Dad was trying to talk Mom into the store-bought kind—a Woolworth's Special. "Really, hon," he insisted. "You're so busy with school. All this work for one day is silly."

I was trying to decide how to handle my eggs. I had swallowed a couple of the larger lumps whole, but a bunch of smaller clumps were still scattered around my plate.

I was afraid Dad might be able to convince Mom to get me a store-bought costume, and I was getting nervous. I pulled some bubble gum out of my pocket and slipped it into my mouth. I'd figure out what to do with my leftover eggs later.

But Mom wouldn't give in. "*No!* No store costume for Murphy. He's our last boy, and I intend to do as much for him as I did for Ken and Tony."

Tony wasn't down for breakfast yet, but Ken was sitting next to me reading the paper while slurping up his cereal. He was so involved in the paper that he wasn't paying attention to anything else. He had finished most of the cereal, but there was still about half a bowl of milk. He kept reading the paper while he went to the cabinet to get the cereal box. That's when I made my move. I quickly mashed up the remaining egg lumps with my fork, made sure Mom and Dad weren't watching, and dumped the eggs into Ken's bowl of milk.

I figured they'd sink. If I was really lucky, they'd dissolve in the bottom of his bowl and he'd never know the difference.

No such luck. I watched out of the corner of my eye as they sank and then popped back to the surface, bobbing lightly as little white blobs on the milk.

I pretended to eat a last bite, scooped up my plate and fork, and dashed to the sink.

Ken sat down, put the paper down, and was ready to pour more cereal into his bowl. "Oh, for crying out loud!" he said. "Look at this milk. It must be sour."

Mom rushed over to look. "It can't be. I just bought it yesterday."

"Well, it's disgusting. It's all curdled in the bowl. That means I must've eaten some. *Blaahch!*" He took the bowl over to the sink and poured the mess out.

"Wait," Dad said. "Let me look at that."

A few lumps were still clinging to the sink, so I quickly took the spray and washed them down the drain.

"Sorry, Dad," I said. "Too late. You didn't want to see it anyway."

Mom was sniffing at the container, insisting it was perfectly good milk. Dad was giving me a strange look. I was anxious to change the subject.

"Ma, could we go down to Woolworth's today and look for a pattern for my costume? Maybe Peter could come with us. That would be fun. You know how much I love to shop with you."

It was a ridiculous thing to say. I hated to shop and she knew it and Dad knew it. But she looked pleased. Besides, I figured that was the only way I could get away from this mess and also have control over my costume. I had to make sure she didn't make me some sissy outfit.

When I called Peter, he was just finishing breakfast. "Sure, Murphy. I'll go with you. Maybe I can get some ideas for Halloween, too."

"That's great," I said. "Listen, Peter. If you've got any extra toast lying around, would you bring it along? Maybe with some peanut butter on it?"

He laughed. "What's the matter? Your dad still cooking?"

"He's a regular madman with a frying pan."

"I'll bring toast, Murphy. Maybe I'll need a favor someday, too."

When we picked Peter up, we both sat in the backseat. I made sure Mom couldn't see me in the rearview mirror as I devoured four pieces of peanut butter toast. Peter kept talking so Mom wouldn't hear me chewing.

At Woolworth's we followed Mom to the sewing department, walking slowly through the aisles that were stuffed with Halloween accessories. We lingered over purple wigs, picked up and tried on fake mustaches, and laughed over gigantic rubber hands and feet. But as soon as I saw the tube of "Dracula blood" and the pair of "authentic plastic fangs" (also dripping with blood), I was hooked.

I left Peter trying on hats and ran to catch up with Mom, who was already studying a pattern book. "Ooh,

Murphy," she said. "Look at this lovely clown outfit with the wonderful ruffled collar."

She turned the page and said, "And look at this cute little bunny costume with the big floppy ears."

I groaned quietly, slipped a piece of gum into my mouth, and just tried to act super bored. I figured old Dracula had to pop up, and sure enough, just before I started to worry that I'd have to be a squirrel, there he was. Big, long black cape with a high stiff collar above the ears. Black vest, and a big red sash. Absolutely super! And with the blood and the fangs—double super!

I started to talk real fast. "That's it, Mom," I shouted. "Dracula." I pointed into the pattern book.

"But, Murphy," Mom said. "That's too common. And it's too easy to make. Now, look at this squirrel—big bushy tail, little ears. I'll even make you a big stuffed nut to carry. You'll look adorable."

Adorable—that was probably the last thing I wanted to look. I had to think fast. "Ma. We have to talk this over seriously. Look—the squirrel would be terrific, but it's not practical." Come on, Murphy, I thought to myself—think. Mom was looking puzzled.

"I, uh, I have to wear the costume in school and the squirrel would be too hot because the heat is always broken and it cranks out ninety degrees even in winter and besides you're so busy with school and all so maybe you better stick to something more simple and besides Dracula is very in and, and . . ." I was losing ground and running out of reasons, not to mention out of breath.

"Murphy, for heaven's sake, slow down." I held my breath while she took a deep one, squeezed her lips together real tight, and knotted up her forehead. Good sign. It was a face that meant she was thinking about giving in. By now I could read her faces pretty well.

"I might consider it, Murphy, except for one thing." Uh-oh, I thought. Come on, brain, don't die on me now. Be ready for anything.

"Dracula does not have beautiful blond hair and you do. It just wouldn't look authentic. Now, let's look at the squirrel."

I looked around in desperation. If I couldn't come up with something, I'd be the nut of our school. I left Mom studying the squirrel costume in the pattern book and ran to find Peter. "Help me, Peter, or I'm going to end up a squirrel." I explained the problem and the two of us started searching through the Halloween department of Woolworth's. I was doomed. I'd have to be sick for Halloween. I'd have to come up with the flu or find a way to be temporarily dying of some dread disease. Anything. No squirrel. Please, God.

He must have heard me. There it was. A can of black and silver sparkle hair spray. Nontoxic. Safe. Easily washed out. One can left and some teenage girl who looked like a punk rocker was reaching for it. I practically had to push her out of the way.

"Scuze me, scuze me," I said quickly. I ducked under her elbow and stood up right in front of her. "It's for my mom. She needs it—bad."

I'm not sure she exactly understood what was happening. Peter was right by my side. "Yeah, his mother," he said. "You know how mothers are." She took a step back and blinked her two-inch black phony eyelashes a few times—real slow. As I took a good look at her, I realized that we had done that girl a favor anyway. She was all dressed in black with long silver fingernails and her hair was done up in spikes sprayed gold. The last thing she needed was silver and black sparkle hair spray. I know it was rude to snatch it from her, but when I'm desperate I don't always know what I'm doing.

We ran back to Mom, bumping into a few people and getting some mighty dirty looks. I was all out of breath by the time I found her—just as she was picking out some gray furry material for the squirrel pattern.

"Mom," I gasped. I could hardly talk, so I started pointing to the can that Peter was holding. She took it from him.

Breath-holding time again. The thinking face again. Then—miracle of miracles—she started to smile. A big, broad smile. "Black hair spray." She chuckled. "Won't that be fun."

I turned to Peter and slapped him a high five. "Thanks, Peter," I said. "Want to come for lunch?"

"Only if you're not having eggs," he said.

CHAPTER FOURTEEN

"Class, I have a *fantastic* new idea," Mrs. Phister said in an excited voice. "We are about to start a *wonderful* new project in the spirit of 'Cooperation.' "

It was two weeks before Halloween and two weeks and one day before the cooperation contest ended. And I had a chance to win two prizes in a row—one for my costume and one for cooperating.

All of us had been cooperating until we were sick of it. We got scoops for being helpful. We got scoops for cleaning up each other's messes. We even got scoops for bringing in cans of food from home for the poor. Ashley and I both brought in so many that we got two scoops each.

In fact, Ashley and I had made a real contest between the two of us. We were way ahead of the rest of the class but always within one scoop of each other. It was getting boring.

But here was Mrs. Phister, with the contest almost

over, thinking of a "wonderful" new idea. I guess she knew we were all getting a little tired of cooperating.

A lot of groans filled the room. Words like *wonderful* and *fantastic* usually meant work, lots of it.

Mrs. Phister kept right on talking, waving her arms excitedly and ignoring the fact that most of us were acting pretty bored. Of course some of the teacher's pets, like Ashley and Jennifer, were pretending to look really interested.

So while Mrs. Phister explained her "wonderful idea," she made sure she was looking right at those girls. "We are all going to work on a library project with a partner. Since we have started to study people who were famous explorers, we will work in groups of two so that we can learn a lot more about them."

Ashley raised her hand. "Oh, Mrs. Phister," she said in a real sweet voice. "That does sound exciting. I'll work with Jennifer or Deanna." Good old Ashley. Always buttering up the teacher.

"Now, hold on, Ashley," said Mrs. Phister. "We are going to let Fate decide the partners. I want a nice mix in these groups. I don't just want friends working together."

But Ashley still wasn't satisfied. "But, Mrs. Phister," she whined. "I might end up with someone dumb. And then I'll be doing all the work. Because I am gifted, you know."

Mrs. Phister was getting annoyed. Ashley had gone too far.

"Ashley," Mrs. Phister said sternly. "That is a *most* unkind and a *most* uncooperative attitude. You may be smart, Ashley. But there is a lot more to being a good person than being smart. You might be wise to also practice a little humility.''

Score two points for Mrs. Phister.

Ashley's cheeks started to get red. Embarrassment? Anger?

You could never be quite sure with Ashley. Anyway, she had enough sense not to answer back. But I heard her mutter under her breath, "I can do almost anything better than anyone in *this* sorry class."

Mrs. Phister looked a little upset, but she put on a cheerful smile and started talking about the project again.

"As I said, class. Fate is going to choose the partners. Who knows what I mean by Fate?"

Iggy Sands raised his hand. "I know, I know," he said, waving his hand in the air. "Fate is something we can't control. When my dad loses money on a horse at the track, he says Fate was against him." We all started to giggle.

"That's an interesting way to define it, Iggy," said Mrs. Phister. "Fate is something we can't control."

She walked to her desk and pulled out a great big chart that had the names of explorers written in all different colors. Names like Christopher Columbus and Magellan and Henry Hudson. Most of them were pretty familiar. A few I had never heard of.

She propped the chart up in front of us and then held up a shoe box. "In this box are twenty-six small colored cubes in thirteen different colors. The colors match the colors of the explorers. When you pull a cube you are choosing an explorer and partner."

81

She started shaking up the box and we could hear the cubes rolling around inside.

She pulled the lid off the box and tilted it so we could see the cubes. Thirteen matching sets of all kinds of colors—including red, green, blue, yellow, white, and black. Then there were ugly-colored cubes of bright orange, sludge brown, pea-soup green, dark purple, and a pink that looked like it could glow in the dark. And all of those colors would determine our explorers and partners for the next two weeks.

She put the lid on once more, shook the box again dramatically, opened it, and we started to pick. One by one she stood next to our desks, held the box over our heads, and allowed us to reach in and pull out a cube.

I was about the fifth kid to pick. I fished into the box and let my fingers run over the cubes, hoping to get a red for Christopher Columbus or a green for Magellan. That would give me a head start, since we had studied those guys last year.

"Hurry up, Murphy," yelled someone behind me. "You can't see the colors, so it doesn't matter." I wrapped my hand around a cube in the corner and pulled it out of the box.

Mrs. Phister moved on. I tried some ESP before I looked. I squeezed my eyes shut and thought *red, red*. Then I peeked into my fist. Pink—bright, ugly, disgusting pink.

I looked up at the chart. Maybe the explorer would still be someone I knew. At first I couldn't even find pink. Then I saw it—way down at the bottom. VASCO DA GAMA was written in big pink letters. I groaned. Anyone with a name like that had to be boring.

The rest of the kids had all picked. Mrs. Phister said, "Okay, everyone. Find your partner." I looked around, hoping Fate had put me with a friend. But Peter had yellow and Greg had white and Michael had pea-soup green.

I looked over at Ashley, wondering if Fate would stick us together, but she was paired up with Iggy Sands. I started to laugh when I saw the look on her face as she realized she'd have to work with Iggy.

But who else had pink? It seemed like there was no one left. I started to think I'd be working alone, when I spotted it. In between the bony little knuckles of Steffie Whiffet I saw a glimpse of pink cube. I strolled over to Steffie's desk and showed her my cube. She barely looked up at me.

Once Mrs. Phister saw that we were all teamed up, she decided it was time to settle down to work.

"Now, class," she said. "We will work with our partners every day for forty minutes for two weeks. Everyone will share reports in front of the room with the whole class. And I expect both partners to share the work."

She paused a minute. "By the way," she continued. "You will also share the grade. Each group will swim together or sink together. If the report is great, both of you will get an A. And if it's poor or if it isn't finished, you will both share an F. Any questions?"

Ashley raised her hand, as usual. "That's not really fair, Mrs. Phister. What if I do all the work?" Ashley knew what it meant to have Iggy as a partner.

Mrs. Phister thought a minute. "Then it's up to you

to get your partner to do some work. The projects must be completed together. Find a creative way to do them if you can. Effort counts. If only one person contributes and presents on the last day, the best the group can hope for is a C. Now get with your partner. You have forty minutes to start planning.''

I knew from the minute I started to talk to Steffie that I was in big trouble. First of all, when it came to schoolwork, she hardly talked. And she wouldn't look at me when I talked to her. I suggested we get some books out of the library.

I could barely hear her answer. ''I don't like to read, Murphy.''

''I'll help you. I'll read to you. Then you can help me write the report.''

''I don't like to write,'' was her answer.

''Then I'll read to you and write, and you can give the report to the class,'' I suggested.

''I won't get up in front of the class,'' she said in a whisper.

She reached into the pocket of her pants and pulled out a small box of crayons. Old stubs of crayons in a ripped and shabby box. Then she pulled a piece of crumpled paper from the other pocket, flattened it on the desk, and started to doodle.

''Steffie,'' I said. ''You've got to pay attention. Mrs. Phister expects a report in two weeks. You want to get an F?''

''It doesn't matter,'' was all she said as she kept coloring away at the paper.

''Come on, Steffie, shape up,'' I hollered. I was trying

84

to shake her up, but I got a little carried away. Mrs. Phister came over.

"Murphy," she said, whispering. "When we work in groups we must use twelve-inch voices. Do you know what that means?"

"Yes, Mrs. Phister," I answered. "My voice shouldn't reach more than twelve inches."

"Right!" she said. "Twelve inches, Murphy. Not twelve feet. Keep that in mind." And she walked away.

Ashley, who was sitting with Iggy near us, leaned over toward me and whispered, "You'll never make it, Murphy."

Mrs. Phister looked up. "Ashley, is there a problem?" she asked.

"Sorry, Mrs. Phister," Ashley answered. "Murphy was just asking me a question." That Ashley, she'd sell her best friend down the river to keep out of trouble.

"Murphy," said Mrs. Phister, raising an eyebrow. "You confine your talking to Steffie. And don't bother other groups."

This definitely was not my day.

CHAPTER FIFTEEN

After a week and a half I was ready to give up. Steffie was impossible to work with, and those forty minutes a day that we spent together felt like forty hours.

Every day at the same time we would sit in our corner. I would drag out the five or six books I had found in the library on Vasco da Gama. Steffie would drag out her raggedy old crayons and a dirty piece of paper. I would talk. Steffie would draw. I would read. Steffie would draw some more.

"Steffie," I finally said. "Listen. We have a report due in a few days. Now, let's get with it. I'll read from this book to you. Take notes."

I read. With lots of enthusiasm to try to get old Steffie interested. I looked up after two pages to see how much she had gotten down on paper. And what did she have? Two ships, a whale, and half a man drawn on the piece of lined paper I had given her to take notes on.

I saw red. I saw an F flash before my eyes. I became a madman. I grabbed the paper and tore it into little pieces.

"Steffie," I said quietly, trying to control my temper. "You're driving me nuts. Please. Just do a little work. And put those lousy crayons away for once, huh?"

Steffie just hung her head and looked sad. "I can't do it," was all she said. "Ask Mrs. Phister for another partner, Murphy. Or maybe she'll let you work alone. It's okay. I won't mind."

I looked at the bits of ripped paper on my desk. "You know, Steffie," I said, "maybe that's not such a bad idea." And I opened a book and tried to read while Steffie went back to drawing on another piece of paper.

I stayed after school to talk to Mrs. Phister. I didn't know what I was going to say, but she had to understand that I couldn't work with Steffie. She had to give me another chance, either with another group or by myself. I knew Ashley was having problems with Iggy; maybe she'd let us switch partners. I could work with Iggy. I could even work with Ashley if I had to. Anyone but Steffie.

I hung around working at my desk until I was sure everyone had left—even the class monitor. Mrs. Phister was putting some papers into her briefcase. "Murphy?" she asked. "Are you still here? Did you want to see me about something?"

I walked slowly to her desk, trying to figure out where to start. "It's about Steffie, Mrs. Phister." And I stopped to think.

"I'm glad you brought that up, Murphy." She came

out from behind her desk and sat at one of our desks. I sat down next to her. "I've been meaning to talk to you about her."

Uh-oh. A red light flashed on in my head. She was going to tell me what a lousy job I was doing with Steffie. I tried to cut her off. "It's been really hard. Steffie doesn't like to work much."

"I know. And I was going to wait until the report was over, but I might as well say it now. I've been watching you work with her. You seem to be doing a fine job. You've been very patient and gentle with her."

I didn't want her to say any more. If she did, I knew I wouldn't be able to ask what I wanted to ask—for a new partner.

But she kept right on talking. "I know a lot of students who would have given up by now. But you've been very understanding of her. You know, in my many years as a teacher, I've come to learn that every child has something very special about them. Even Steffie. Students like you help a lot."

"Thanks, Mrs. Phister." What else could I say?

She continued, "Yes, people like you and Ashley can do a lot for someone like Steffie."

"Ashley?" I know I sounded shocked, but Ashley hadn't been Steffie's number one supporter that I could ever see.

"Yes—Ashley. Does that surprise you?"

This conversation was getting complicated. "I guess not. Not really. It's just that I never thought of Ashley and Steffie as friends."

"I'm not sure I would call them friends. But I do

know that Ashley helps Steffie with her schoolwork once in a while. Ashley's very bright, you know.''

"I know." This whole conversation had not gone the way I had planned. Not only could I not ask for another partner. Now I had to hear how Ashley was such a big help. I don't know why, but it just seemed to add to the pressure.

"But enough of that, Murphy. What did you want to see me about?"

"Nothing important. I just hope you're not expecting great things from Steffie and me. Vasco's a pretty dull guy."

She smiled. "I *always* expect great things from you, Murphy. I guess that's part of the price you pay for being gifted."

Oh swell! Who needed it? If I was so gifted, how come I didn't feel smart?

CHAPTER SIXTEEN

I went to school the next morning with a new determination. I knew it was the last day we would be able to work since tomorrow was Halloween and we had an all-day party planned. And I knew we wouldn't be able to make an A report in only forty minutes. But I also knew that somehow I had to try to get Steffie to work; I wanted to live up to Mrs. Phister's good opinion of me.

Mrs. Phister hustled us into our groups right after we pledged the flag. "This is your last chance, class. You should be putting the finishing touches on your reports. Try to make them special."

Finishing touches? How about starting touches? We hadn't even gotten ours off the ground. Forget special. But I wasn't going to get myself discouraged. I had to get Steffie moving.

When we got together, Steffie was even more quiet

than usual. She seemed a little nervous. Maybe she thought I was going to yell at her. I tried a new approach. "Hi, Steffie. You know, I really have enjoyed working with you. Let's see if we can get something done today—together."

She seemed to relax a little. In other words, she took her crayons out and started drawing.

"Hey, Steff," I said, trying to put the big-time excitement into my voice. "Wait till you hear what I found out about old Vasco. It'll knock you over."

She was deep into her coloring. "Um-hmmm," was her answer.

"Steffie. Listen. Really. Vasco da Gama had some pretty scary adventures. He even fought pirates. We could do a great report."

"That's nice," she muttered, still coloring.

I started to read from the book. I made it all sound very dramatic and I read very slowly, hoping Steffie would listen. I read about how Vasco da Gama sailed from Portugal south to Africa in ships that were smaller than Columbus's. I read about how he was one of the first traders in South Africa, exchanging little bells and scarlet red caps for white ivory bangles. I read how he even traded for an ox that he brought on his ship so his men could have fresh meat. And I also read how he was embarrassed when he finally sailed around Africa to India because the stuff he brought to trade for spices in India looked like junk compared to all the riches of India.

After twenty minutes of reading and talking excitedly,

I said, "What do you think, Steffie? Neat stuff, huh?"

Steffie never even looked up. She was working away with those crayons and a whole bunch of scraps of paper. I swear she never even heard a word of what I had said.

Suddenly I felt tired. And sad. And useless. And it wasn't because I thought we'd fail the report. It was something else. It was like I had somehow failed for Steffie.

I put my elbows on the desk, rested my chin in my hands, and stared at the desk. My eyes fell on Steffie's drawing and I watched blankly as her crayon colored on the paper.

Then all of a sudden I started to look hard at what she was doing. I grabbed the paper out from under her stubby red crayon.

I could hardly believe my eyes. There in front of me was a terrific little picture of two men exchanging red caps and ivory bangles.

I grabbed for the small pile of papers on Steffie's desk. It was all there in picture form. Vasco fighting pirates, ships sailing along a coast, an ox on board a ship. Even a picture of Vasco looking all red-faced as he tried to trade his goods in India.

"Steffie," I said, really excited this time. "These pictures. They're fantastic. They're beautiful. They show everything I read to you just now. And some of these are from stuff I read on the other days."

And believe me, I wasn't exaggerating. They were

small and all folded up, and some of the paper was scruffy around the edges. But they were the greatest pictures I had ever seen. "How come you never showed these to me before?"

She reached for the pictures, but I pulled them behind me. "Don't make fun of me. Please. Don't show anybody."

"What do you mean, don't show anybody?" I was getting annoyed. "You can really draw."

She looked at me and must have realized I was being serious. She started to explain in a real quiet voice. "I feel good when I draw. When you read, I see pictures in my head. Then I feel like I have to draw them. I like the way you read. You make real bright pictures dance through my mind."

"And then through your fingers onto paper," I said. I was amazed. I was feeling terrific. "This is it, Steffie. We'll get some bigger paper. We'll get you a whole bunch more crayons. You draw. I'll write." Visions of an A started to dance through my head.

Mrs. Phister's voice cut through that vision. "Five more minutes, class. Finish up quickly. You've all worked hard. I'm excited to see the reports day after tomorrow. And I also can't wait to see all your costumes for Halloween tomorrow."

I turned to Steffie. "We're running out of time. Tell you what. I'll write the report tonight. You do those pictures bigger at home."

"I can't," was all she said.

"What do you mean, you can't?" I asked.

"My father won't let me color at home. He says it's a waste of time."

"Tell him it's homework," I said.

She got that really sad-eyed look. "He won't believe me. I'm not going to do it. He just gets mad at me."

I couldn't believe it. All that talent going to waste on scraps of paper and stubby crayons in school. Then I got another great idea. "Wait here."

I walked up to Mrs. Phister's desk. "Scuze me, ma'am," I said in my sweetest voice.

"Yes, Murphy?"

"Well, it's like this," I began. "Steffie and I aren't quite finished. We're going to have a dynamite report. But we need one more day to give it real pizzazz. Could we work on it one more day and be a little late?" I thought, after yesterday's talk, that she'd probably say yes. She thought awhile before she answered. "I'm sorry, Murphy. But if I give you an extension, everyone else will be entitled to one also. I'm sure your report will have more than enough pizzazz."

I shuffled back to my desk. What report, I thought. "We're doomed, Steffie," I said. "I'll do a report. At least we'll get a C."

"I'm sorry," she said. "You got stuck with a lousy partner." And I knew she meant it.

I spent the rest of the morning thinking about it. I knew I had to forget it. I knew there was nothing else I could do. But my mind wouldn't let it go.

By lunchtime my brain had worked overtime. I had another idea. But I had to be careful how I presented it.

I didn't want Steffie—or anyone else—to get the wrong idea. I found Steffie sitting with Ashley and her friends.

"Steffie," I said. "Could I talk to you a minute? Alone?" Ashley gave me a funny look. "About our report," I said, loud enough for everyone to hear.

She came over to a corner with me. "Listen, Steffie. We've got a chance to do a great report. With your talent and my brains, we could knock this class off its feet."

She stood quietly listening.

"Can you come over to my house this afternoon? I don't mean walk home with me—I have to jog with my dad after school. But later. Like about an hour after school?"

She thought for a while and then said, "I guess so, Murphy."

I suddenly got excited. "That's great. You'll see. It'll be terrific. Trust me. I know what I'm doing."

I guess I was too excited, because all the girls at Ashley's table had turned around and were looking at us. So I said extra loud, "Yes, Steffie. You're right. It'll be a great report on Vasco da Gama."

After lunch Mrs. Phister reminded us again that our reports were due the day after Halloween. "And another thing," she said. "Since that will also be the last day of our 'Catch-a-Kid' contest, the team with the best report will each be awarded the final scoop."

Ashley leaned over and whispered, "Well, you gave it your best, Murphy. But like I've been telling you all along, you can't always be a winner. Be nice to me, and I'll let you come for ice cream when I win."

I turned around and looked at the back board. Ashley had one more scoop than me. And I knew she was counting on me not getting a scoop before the report. That would mean that whether she and Iggy won or not, she'd still be the winner by one scoop.

I leaned close to her and whispered back, "Don't count your scoops till they're hatched, Ashley. You could get licked."

I was enjoying myself. "Get it, Ashley? Licked?"

I knew I was feeling better, because when I feel good, I have this terrific sense of humor.

CHAPTER SEVENTEEN

After my jog, I was a nervous wreck. What if Steffie didn't come? What if she got here and didn't want to work? Life sure was complicated.

The doorbell rang.

"Hi, Steffie," I said, suddenly embarrassed. I didn't want her to think I was too anxious to have her over. I didn't want her to get the wrong idea. After all, our relationship was strictly business.

I introduced Steffie to Mom and then showed her into the family room. She sat in a chair at the table and looked like she was lost.

"Steffie," I said, "I've got something to show you."

But she didn't move from her chair. She was deep into concentrating on a fingernail she was picking at.

"Steffie," I said a little louder. "You with me? Hello?

Steffie?'' I walked over to her and waved my hand in front of her nose.

She stopped picking her fingernail but didn't look up. Mom asked if we wanted cookies and milk, but I quickly said, "No, thanks. We won't be long. It's just some schoolwork we have to finish."

I brought over the supplies. I had huge sheets of clean white drawing paper that I talked Mom into letting me use. And I had my own brand-new set of crayons—the sixty-four-color variety.

Steffie was still staring at the table, so I slid them all under her nose. I also figured it was time for a speech. "Listen, Steffie," I started. "This is not a social call. This is a business meeting. We have a report due. Now, let's cut the nonsense and—"

She didn't let me finish, and I was giving a great speech. "Where did you get such beautiful paper?" She was running her hand over it like it was silk. "And all these crayons? Are they yours? They're brand-new."

"Yeah. Well, I got them when one of my relatives came for a visit. Seems they always bring me crayons. I'm not much into coloring."

But Steffie had tuned out on me again. She had spread the crayons out on the table, pulled one of her ragged sketches out of her pocket, and was drawing away like mad.

"Listen, Steffie. I'll be right here working on the report if you need me for anything." But I don't even think she realized I was around. I have never seen anyone look so happy and so intense as Steffie did with that paper and those crayons.

Once she interrupted me and said, "Murphy, read that part to me again about the pirates. I want to see the pictures in my head again." And I stopped and read until she said, "Okay, that's enough." Then we both got back to work.

By the time I finished writing, Steffie had knocked out ten really dynamite pictures plus a full-colored map of Vasco da Gama's explorations. Mom and Dad came in to see our work.

"Steffie," Mom said excitedly. "These are so beautiful. I can't believe you did them so quickly."

Dad added, "They look positively professional. Steffie, you have a wonderful future in art."

Steffie was smiling a bigger smile than I had ever seen. "Do you really like them?"

Dad laughed. "Like them? I think they're fantastic!"

Steffie looked down at her drawings and nodded slightly. "Yeah. They are pretty good, huh?" And she looked proudly at each of us.

When Mom said, "Who's ready for a snack?" Steffie and I both raised our hands. Dad brought in a big bowl of fruit, and while Steffie and I munched on apples, we talked about our project. By the time Steffie was ready to leave, she had said more than she had all year.

As she was leaving, Steffie came over to me and said, "Do you think Ashley will like my drawings, too, Murphy?"

Now, that annoyed me. "What do you care what Ashley thinks? She's a jerk."

She almost got mad again. "I don't know why you don't like Ashley. She can be very nice. You just have to understand her."

I guess she was right—maybe. But what she thought of Ashley didn't matter. I was feeling so good about our report that I thought I might bust. Tomorrow I'd win a prize for Dracula and the next day Steffie would help me win one with Vasco. What more could I ask for?

CHAPTER EIGHTEEN

"Murphy, this stuff is *sticky!* It's going to get all over everything."

"Keep spraying, Mom. You missed a little spot over there."

It was Halloween morning and I was straining to see as much of my black sparkly hair as I could in the bathroom mirror. Mom was holding the hair spray with one hand and her nose with the other.

What a great day!

"No—no more. That's enough. We'll never get this goo out of your hair. It's drying like gum."

I took the can from her and gave my hair one last squirt.

"Thanks, Mom," I said, giving her a quick hug.

She touched my hair with one finger and made a face. "I still think your cape is too long."

That was the only argument we had while she was making it. "The cape is too long," she had said. "Much too long. It drags on the floor. I'll have to shorten it.''

But I had insisted. "It's more dramatic this way. I can whip it around and pull it up in front of my face. Don't shorten it. Please?" I didn't want to be a Dracula with a high-water cape.

It took about twenty more "pleases," but she finally gave in. "Well, okay. Just make sure you don't step on it. It could rip."

She kept fussing with my hair, pushing down the stiff strands that kept popping up. "You won't have any trouble putting on your costume in school, will you?"

"I'm not a little kid. Besides, all the guys help each other." I gave her another hug. "Thanks for making me such a great costume. I'll probably win first prize."

She looked skeptical. "It's really not a fancy costume. There's not a lot to it. Don't be disappointed if you don't win."

Just like Mom. She never wanted me to get hurt, so she spent a lot of time "preparing" me for the worst. But I knew she was proud of the costume—after all, she had made me try it on three different times, just to make sure it looked okay.

"Honest, Mom. Don't worry. Nothing can possibly go wrong today!"

What a great day!

Peter and I were so excited about Halloween that we couldn't even eat breakfast. We ran all the way to school.

Of course everyone had something to say about my

black hair. Everyone wanted to touch it, and I felt like I was swatting flies to keep everyone's hands off me.

Ashley thought she was a real comedian. "Oh, Murphy," she said in a real phony, sophisticated voice. "What happened? Did you fall in a grease puddle on your way to school? Or are you supposed to be a fly who got banged with a flyswatter? Your hair looks like squashed fly juice." And she giggled and touched my hair with the tips of her fingers. Ashley—what a dumb girl. I couldn't wait to see her dumb old costume.

Mrs. Phister just looked at me and said in some kind of foreign accent, "Interesting, Murphy. Very interesting." Then she tried to cackle like she was Dracula or a witch or something. I was surrounded by female comedians.

We couldn't wait for the morning routine to be over. Right after attendance and the national anthem, we all ran to the gym to the locker rooms to get dressed. I smeared the white makeup all over my face and added big gobs of fake blood around my mouth. I used eyebrow pencil to blacken my eyebrows and I added a big black scar on my cheek. What a great day!

When I was done, I looked for my friends. Greg was dressed in a karate outfit with a headband and his eyes made up like he was Chinese. Michael told us he was a rock star. He was wearing black clothes with a lot of tinfoil attached and a pair of funky sunglasses. But he didn't have a guitar or anything, so it was hard to tell.

Peter had dressed up like a bum with a big pillow stuffed around his belly, a floppy hat, and baggy pants with red suspenders. We all punched his stomach, and when we pulled our fists out, it left a big dent. It took us a few minutes to fluff him back into shape.

We walked around the locker room, checking everyone out. There were monsters in assorted shapes and sizes, some soldiers, a kid who had cut holes in a sheet for a ghost, a clown, a lot of store-bought costumes, and a bunch that didn't really look like much of anything. But I guess they knew what they were supposed to be.

There were even a few other Draculas. Each time I saw one I checked myself in the nearest mirror. You're the best, Murphy, old kid, I thought as I slipped my fangs into my mouth and hissed at my reflection. I almost scared myself. Good thing I knew it was me.

Then we spotted Raymond Stubbs. He had on a plain pair of dirty pants and a big old used-to-be-white T-shirt. "Raymond," Peter said, coming up next to him. "What're you supposed to be?"

"I'm a commando, Peter. Look!" He pointed to a few holes in his T-shirt. "I been shot up."

"Listen, Raymond," I said. "I got a good idea. I've got this fake blood. Want to use some? I'm done with it."

"Yeah, Murph. Can I?" So I opened my tube and wrote in blood on the front of his T-shirt, "I BEEN SHOT." Then he turned around and Peter wrote "UP" on his back in big bloody letters. He loved it. It took my whole tube of blood, but it was worth it the way Raymond kept turning around and around to see himself in the mirror.

When we were all done, we ran out into the gym to meet up with the girls for the parade. They were really something to see—some were dressed like fairies and princesses and ballerinas, prancing around and posing. Then there were witches and karate girls and superheroes like Wonder Woman. When I spotted Ashley, I almost fell over myself laughing.

Ashley was wearing a squirrel suit like the one my mom had tried to talk me into. Only difference was, her suit had a little frilly yellow skirt around the waist and a bow in her big tail.

I couldn't resist. I walked over to her and whispered, "You make a lovely nut, Ashley. In fact, you're about as nuts as they come." A couple of the other guys had heard me, and we all started laughing. Then I whipped my cape around a few times, practically hitting Ashley in the face. I pulled the cape up to my eyes, glared at Ashley, and said in a deep Dracula voice. "I vill drink squirrel blood." Then I snapped my cape near her nose a few times.

I could tell she wasn't amused. She lowered her eyebrows, stared at me, and said, "You just wait, Murphy Darinzo. Before this day is over, you'll be sorry." And that just made me laugh harder at her.

"Nuts to you, Ashley." I was really in top form.

Then she turned around and made sure her big old bushy tail, which stuck straight up, hit me in the face.

Mr. Petersen, our gym teacher, blew on his whistle a couple of times and, with the help of the other teachers, we finally got lined up for the big parade. Ashley ended up right behind me, and I made sure to flap my cape just to annoy her a little more.

We walked out into the beautiful October day, lined

up by grades, and started marching in a big circle around the field. A few of the teachers stood at the far end, acting as the judges for the best costumes. At least five kids from each grade would be given a card as they passed the judges. Then they would line up for the final judging. And one kid from each grade would get "Best Costume of the Year" and get a picture in the paper. I had won for the last few years and hoped I had a chance to win again. What a great day!

I got a card on the first round, and so did Ashley. As I held my card, I heard a teacher say, "All right, children. Circle the field once more. Time for the final judging."

I started off with Ashley right behind me again. I kept flipping my cape up at her and I knew I was getting on her nerves because she kept saying, "Cut it out, Murphy. Stop it."

We were making the last turn and coming down the field when suddenly I felt a big yanking at my neck, like someone was choking me. Then I heard a gigantic *R-R-R-I-I-P-P*. I turned around fast. And I couldn't believe it. Ashley was standing on my cape. Most of it was on the ground. Some of it was dangling from my neck.

"Ashley," I screamed. "What do you think you're doing?"

She looked at me with big innocent eyes. "Gee, I'm sorry. Looks like I stepped on your cape by accident."

"What do you mean, 'accident'? Any dope can see you did it on purpose."

"No, I didn't," she said. "I was just walking regular, and your cape got under my foot. It was too long."

I thought she was smiling a little, but I couldn't be sure. "Better luck next time, Murphy. It *was* a nice costume." And she flipped her tail into my face and walked down the field, where the rest of the kids were waiting.

I picked up my cape and slumped off to the side. I guess Mom was right. I guess the cape was too long. But I also guess that was no accident.

I watched from the sidelines as the winners were announced—including Ashley Douglas. Right up there on the judge's platform for the whole school to see.

Steffie came over and stood next to me while Ashley, still on the platform, twirled round and round, showing off. "Aren't you just thrilled for Ashley?" Steffie asked.

"Oh, yeah, just thrilled."

Steffie was too wrapped up in watching Ashley get her prize to notice that I was being sarcastic.

Everyone was calling her costume "creative, original, one-of-a-kind." Next time I'll listen to Mom. Maybe.

What a lousy day!

CHAPTER NINETEEN

I might have gotten really depressed about Halloween except for two things. Mom fixed up my cape and I had a great time trick-or-treating with Peter and Michael and Greg. And second, the next day was our report, and I knew Steffie and I would win. I had a lot to look forward to.

Mom drove me to school because I had to bring in the drawings and the report as well as my usual school stuff. She gave me a quick kiss (she knows I'm not into kissing in public) and said, "Good luck. You and Steffie really did a super job."

When I got into class, I looked around for Steffie, but she wasn't there yet. In fact, when the first bell rang, she still hadn't shown up.

Ashley must have noticed, too. "Tough luck, Murphy," she said, grinning. "Looks like your partner deserted you. Get set to lose."

I know I should have ignored her, but she always

managed to get me going. "Lose what, Ashley? You're the only loser I see around here."

Her voice got a little deeper. "Oh, yeah? Well, let's not forget who won yesterday. And take a look at the back board, Mr. Marvelous Murphy. I'm one scoop ahead of you, and this project ends the contest. So, unless you come up with a miracle, I am the clear winner—again." She paused a minute and then added, "Which I told you I would be all along, by the way."

"The day's still not over, Ashley, old girl," I said, trying to top her cool confidence which, under the circumstances, was not easy to do. But I kept looking around for Steffie.

She walked in five minutes after the pledge to the flag with a note excusing her tardiness. As she stood next to Mrs. Phister's desk, all the kids were staring at her. She was wearing a dress for the first time ever, a pretty dress. Her hair was all clean and shiny. She looked so great that one of the guys in the back of the room whistled.

For the first time Steffie didn't look like she wanted to melt into the background. She was standing taller and prouder than usual, smiling happily as she talked with Mrs. Phister.

As soon as we were all settled down, the reports began. The first few were okay, but a little boring. Ashley and Iggy did Magellan, the explorer who was the first to go around the world. They included a little skit in which Iggy played Magellan. He danced around the whole room (which was supposed to be the world, I guess) while Ashley read the report. Not bad, except that Iggy couldn't keep from fooling around and Ashley finally yelled at him to be serious. That just made Iggy fool around more. Ashley read that Magellan died before he finished the voyage, so his crew had to finish it for him. Iggy put on a hysterical dying scene that made all of us laugh and made Ashley want to kill Iggy.

By the time they were done, I thought Ashley was going to go over and smack Iggy off the head. But she just turned to Mrs. Phister and said in a real syrupy voice, "We worked extra hard, Mrs. Phister. In fact, I think you'll see that we worked harder than almost anyone else in this room." And she looked over at me and grinned. Then she faced the class and took a bow. I couldn't believe it. She was actually waiting for people to applaud her. And a couple of people did—including Deanna and Jennifer. Even Steffie started to applaud, but a look from me made her stop.

We were up next. I had the drawings in a big black plastic garbage bag so no one would see them until we were ready. As I brought the bag up front, Ashley whispered, "We're ready for your garbage report, Murphy." This time I ignored her.

Steffie and I stood in front of the room. As I started to read the report—with all the feeling and excitement I could put in my voice—Steffie pulled her first drawing out of the bag and held it up.

I could hear the amazement from the class. "Wow . . . oooh . . . look at that . . . that's beautiful." In fact, they were so caught up in the drawings, I didn't think they heard much of my report. Except for Mrs. Phister.

110

I glanced over at her and she was smiling so big I thought her face would crack.

When we finished, Steffie packed the pictures back in the bag. And suddenly everyone started to applaud. It was a terrific feeling. Steffie blushed a little, but I knew how happy and proud she was.

After the rest of the reports were done, everyone started to crowd around Steffie, asking to see the pictures again. Even Ashley came over and started making a big fuss. "Steffie," she said. "I didn't know you were so talented. And I love your outfit. Tell me where you got it. Maybe you can come over to my house some afternoon."

Then she turned to me and said, "Nice job, Murphy. You and Steffie had a great report." That surprised me a little. I didn't think Ashley could be so nice.

Mrs. Phister asked Steffie if it would be all right if she hung her pictures on the back bulletin board once the scoops were down. It was probably the best day Steffie had all year. And it made me feel good to be such a big part of it.

When it came time to award the scoops for the best project, Steffie and I naturally won. As Mrs. Phister handed me my scoop, I realized that this put me in a tie with Ashley. Not quite a win, but at least she hadn't beaten me. The way I figured it, we would split the prize, but we didn't have to share it. Each of us could take one friend for ice cream—on different days, of course. I looked over at Ashley, figuring she'd be steaming, but it didn't seem to bother her too much. In fact, she looked over at me and smiled.

Suddenly Steffie raised her hand. Mrs. Phister looked surprised, because Steffie had never ever raised her hand before.

"Yes, Steffie?" she asked.

Steffie stood up, holding her scoop. She turned to the class and said, "I would like to give my scoop to someone else, if that would be all right."

"That's a most unusual request," Mrs. Phister said. "You worked very hard to earn it."

"That's okay," answered Steffie. "I'd like to give it away."

I could hardly believe it. I was going to beat Ashley after all. I held my breath as Mrs. Phister stood there thinking.

Mrs. Phister looked at me for a second. And then she looked at Steffie. My fate was really in her hands now, and I think she knew it. "All right, Steffie. But only because you worked so hard on the report."

Ashley raised her hand. When Mrs. Phister ignored her, Ashley waved it frantically in the air. "Mrs. Phister, I don't think it's fair to break the rules. The contest ended in a tie, and I think it should stay that way. Murphy and I will have to share the prize."

"I'm sorry, Ashley," Mrs. Phister said politely. "I think I will allow Steffie the privilege of giving such a hard-earned scoop away."

Steffie stood up. I was looking down at my desk, trying to act humble, so I didn't realize what happened until it was all over.

Steffie walked right past my desk and said, "Ashley, I want to give this to you."

I looked up, shocked. There was Steffie, handing her scoop over to Ashley. There was Ashley, also looking shocked, but also reaching out to take the scoop. I looked at Mrs. Phister, who was also looking shocked—I think.

Mrs. Phister said, "Steffie. Why Ashley?"

Ashley didn't even wait for Steffie to speak. "Because we're such good friends, Mrs. Phister. That's why." And she walked to the back of the room and stuck her last scoop up. One scoop higher than mine.

Ashley turned around and faced the class, hands on her hips, looking extremely pleased. She looked around and noticed that everyone was looking at her very quietly. She also noticed Steffie, who was still standing by Ashley's desk.

It seemed like hours passed as Ashley watched us and we watched her. No one said a word. Suddenly Ashley turned around, unpinned her top scoop, and moved it over on top of my cone. "I don't deserve this, Mrs. Phister. Murphy does. He's the one who did the report with Steffie. I didn't. And fair is fair." She went back to her desk and sat down.

It didn't take me long to figure out why Steffie had given Ashley the scoop. She knew if I won or even if we tied, I wouldn't have asked Ashley—even if I wanted to. But she also knew that if Ashley won, she'd ask me. I think Steffie was trying to get us together.

Mrs. Phister was looking totally confused. I figured it was time to add to her confusion. I stood in front of the class and said, "Mrs. Phister, I'd like to tell everyone who I'm taking to share my prize. I'm going to take my

113

good friends Peter and Michael and Greg.'' The three of them cheered. ''And I'm also taking Steffie and Ashley.''

''But, Murphy,'' Mrs. Phister said, ''the prize at The Sundae School is only for four.''

''That's okay,'' I answered. ''I've got some extra money saved. Besides, with six of us, it'll be a real party.''

I was feeling very generous. Maybe Steffie was right to give the scoop to Ashley. It sure had forced Ashley to act nicer. And it had certainly forced Ashley to give it to the person who had deserved it all along—me!

CHAPTER TWENTY

When I slammed my way through the front door after school, Mom was standing in the kitchen. "Murphy," she said. "Slow down. You're going to take the door off its hinges one of these days."

"Where's Dad?" I asked, all out of breath. "I have something to tell both of you. Then Dad and I have to jog."

She looked at me strangely. "He called to say he'd be late. He told me to tell you that you could skip a day of jogging."

"No way. I'm on a program, you know." She followed me up to my room and, as I changed into my workout clothes, I told her all about Steffie and the report and how I won the "Catch-a-Kid" contest. I didn't tell her that I was also taking Steffie and Ashley when I got my prize. That would take too long to explain.

She was really happy for me and I stopped to give her a big hug just before I flew back out the front door.

"That reminds me," she said, holding on to me so I'd have to listen. "You had a phone call. From Ashley. She wanted to know about your date."

I groaned. "Figures."

She held me tighter. "What date, Murphy? Since when are you *dating?* Don't you think you're a little young for a date? Why, I didn't date until—"

I cut her off. "Don't worry about it, Mom. Honest. It's not a date. Don't listen to Ashley. She just gets funny ideas into her head. Listen. I've got to go. Tell Dad I went jogging. I'll explain it all later."

As I started to run my laps on the track, I thought about all the things that had happened. I thought about Steffie and how proud she looked standing up in front of the class. I thought about Ashley and wondered if I'd ever understand her. And I thought about my good friends Peter and Michael and Greg and how lucky I was.

Before I knew it, I had run two laps and I wasn't even tired. Not a pain in my body. I saw Dad coming and waited for him.

"You came up to jog all by yourself," he said, sounding a little surprised.

"Yeah, Dad. I didn't know what time you'd be home, so I came up to do my laps. I just finished."

He looked a little disappointed. "Good boy, Murphy. I'll meet you home. Then we can talk."

I thought for a minute. "Dad, would you mind if I ran with you for a while? I feel pretty good and I'd like to try for a mile. If that's okay with you."

He looked like I had handed him a present. As we jogged together I told him all about Steffie and the contest.

As we started the last lap of the mile, Dad looked at me and said, "Murphy?"

"Yeah, Dad?"

"I like you, Murphy."

"Thanks, Dad. I like you, too."

He was quiet for a while, then said again, "Murphy?"

"Yeah, Dad?"

A long silence. Then, "I have a big favor to ask, Murphy."

"Anything for you, Dad. You name it."

Another long silence. This was going to be a tough one, I could tell.

As we rounded the last turn he said, "Would you mind terribly if I didn't cook your breakfast anymore? I'm getting awfully tired of trying to find new ways to make egg whites exciting."

We both stopped running and I turned to face my father. Trying hard to keep a straight face, I said, "Anything for you. It'll be hard, but anything for you."

"You're a good kid, Murphy Darinzo," he said, wiping the sweat off my face with his towel.

"I take after you, Dad," I said. "Come on. Let's run another lap."

About the Author

M. M. RAGZ is the writing coordinator for Stamford High School in Stamford, Connecticut. She literally does her writing on the run, developing story ideas while jogging five miles a day. While her job with the school system keeps her busy teaching writing, conducting writing workshops and seminars, and giving book talks, Mrs. Ragz occupies her free time with a range of activities that includes watercolor painting, crafts, gardening, and summers on Cape Cod in Eastham. She holds three college degrees from the University of Connecticut and Fairfield University. She has traveled to Germany, Mexico, Greece, Britain, and the Carribbean.

She lives in Trumbull, Connecticut, with her husband and their youngest son, Michael, who is the inspiration for many of Murphy's adventures.